S0-BHU-748

The New Adventures of The MAD SCIENTISTS' CLUB

by the author of
THE MAD SCIENTISTS' CLUB

The New Adventures

Illustrated by Charles Geer

of the

MAD SCIENTISTS' CLUB

Bertrand R. Brinley

PURPLE HOUSE PRESS
Texas

Published by
Purple House Press, Ltd. Co.
1625 Village Trail, Keller, TX 76248

Library of Congress Cataloging-in-Publication Data

Brinley, Bertrand R.
The new adventures of the mad scientists' club / by Bertrand R. Brinley ; illustrated by Charles Geer.
p. cm.
Summary: The seven members of the Mad Scientists' Club experiment with new projects which include making rain and launching a flying saucer.
ISBN 1-930900-11-2 (alk. paper)
[1. Science clubs–Fiction.] I. Geer, Charles, ill. II. Title.
PZ7.B78013 Ne 2002
[Fic]–dc21 2002002366

www.PurpleHousePress.com

Printed in the United States of America
1 2 3 4 5 6 7 8 9 10
First Edition

The New Adventures of
The MAD SCIENTISTS' CLUB

Introduction

Somewhere beyond our daily cares lies a town with a quaint square in its center. The square is enclosed by old brick buildings with awnings offering shade to shoppers and strollers. The trees around the square are tall and ample in their maturity.

Now, in the soft light of the early evening, a group of young boys gathers together. Snatches of their talk drift across the square, telling of adventures just completed and of others yet to come.

Our young band of adventurers is about to embark on what became the second collection of stories about the Mad Scientists of Mammoth Falls which my father wrote. They find themselves encountering situations that prove more complex and dangerous than their escapades in the tales that first brought them to readers' attention.

Their curiosity—a hallmark of all scientists—gets them into trouble with criminals. They fulfill a dream many of us have, when they refit a midget submarine and mysteriously relocate it to a hidden cavern. And they apply some practical science when they become rain-makers during a hot, dry summer in Mammoth Falls.

The rainmaker story has an interesting twist in its history. It was supposed to be the eighth tale in *The Mad Scientists' Club* book; but the editor rejected it and the book was published with seven stories. Some months afterwards, the publisher wrote my father, complimenting him on the story and urging that it be included in the volume you now have.

Between tracking criminals and coaxing rain out of clouds, our imaginative band still finds time to pull off a prank or two on the townspeople and settle accounts with the notorious Harmon Muldoon.

But there are some surprises awaiting the club members. Harmon proves himself more resourceful than they think. They also find themselves embroiled in some town politics—a harbinger of things to come—when their rainmaking is too successful.

These tales were written over a period of four years, the chronology being:

Big Chief Rainmaker
The Telltale Transmitter
The Cool Cavern
The Flying Sorcerer
The Great Confrontation

They all involved research, as did the first seven stories. In one case, I like to think that the idea for the midget submarine that figures in *The Cool Cavern* originated in Japan. When we lived in Tokyo in the 1950s, we visited the big port at Yokohama and the naval base at Yokosuka frequently. At the latter, a captured midget submarine was on display. I clambered in and around it one day while my parents ran some errands at the base. As the day wore on and they did not show up, I became a bit concerned that something had happened or perhaps they had forgotten where they left me. Much to my relief, they did return finally and pick me up. But I can't believe that the sub was not firmly planted in my father's memory after this episode.

While researching the story, he obtained photostats

of declassified Office of Naval Intelligence publications that had descriptions of Japanese midget submarines. One of these subs was the "Pearl Harbor" type, named for one that was beached on Oahu Island on December 7, 1941. This sub was forty-one feet in length and five feet across, with a four-and-a-half foot tall conning tower. My guess is that this was the model for the midget sub the club members refurbish and then hide in the underwater cavern.

In another story, the hero is not one of the Mad Scientists, but a German shepherd dog named Kaiser Bill. Kaiser Bill was our first family dog, whom we purchased in Germany as a puppy and called "Bobo." Bobo went everywhere the family did: Austria, Massachusetts, New Jersey, California, Japan, Panama and New York. Kaiser Bill does everything—with a few exaggerations here and there—that Bobo did.

Kaiser Bill's owner, Zeke Boniface, appears again with his mythical truck, Richard the Deep Breather. They play an important part in *The Flying Sorcerer*, which was suggested by the publicity UFOs were getting in the Fifties and Sixties. I suspect my father had many times dreamed of how much fun it would be to fly something resembling a flying saucer and raise havoc with the local citizenry and the Air Force. He knew that geodesic structures are quite light and strong, and that they are pretty easy to build. Add the Mad Scientists, and you are on your way to another adventure.

This story appears in its proper sequence, as does *The Great Confrontation*—which is the last short story about the Mad Scientists of Mammoth Falls; the others were arranged in the order you encounter them for editorial reasons. We have, as we did in *The Mad Scientists' Club*, left them in the original sequence.

As the Milky Way blankets the sky and town with luminescent starlight, small stars dance on the low horizon. They seem to soar up and then dash off, driven by the wind. Are they really celestial lights or a trick of the imagination? Turn the pages of this book and you will learn the answer as you are transported into the realm of the imagination with the Mad Scientists of Mammoth Falls.

Sheridan Brinley
Arlington, Virginia
2002

Contents

The Telltale Transmitter

Henry Mulligan has always had a generous supply of what is called scientific curiosity. Sometimes it gets us into trouble—like the time Freddy Muldoon and Dinky Poore got kidnapped for being too nosey about something Henry had discovered.

Henry is a great one for thinking ahead, and he always has some new project planned for the Mad Scientists' Club to work on during vacation periods. Last Easter we had about ten days off from school, and he was all ready for it with a carefully thought-out program to study earth tremors in the vicinity of Mammoth Falls. We spent the first couple of days building seismographs that Henry had designed and calibrating them in our clubhouse in Jeff Crocker's barn. It isn't very difficult to build a good seismograph. Knowing what to do with it is something else.

Most scientific projects boil down to two things: some serious thinking and a lot of hard work. In the Mad Scientists' Club we split it up evenly. Henry and Jeff do most of the thinking, and the rest of us do the work.

The seismograph project was no exception. Henry had figured out just where he wanted to place the instruments so that we could develop a good record of the pattern of earth movements around the Mammoth Falls area. He decided that we should keep one in the clubhouse in Jeff's barn and make it the central recording station where he and Jeff would analyze all the data we got. The other three instruments we built would be placed at three distant points, so as to form a large triangle with the town in the center.

Naturally, Henry had picked out three places that were hard to get to. But as I said, he and Jeff only had to do the thinking. The rest of us had to set up the field instruments and then trek out to each one of them every day to change the graph paper on the recording drums and bring the last day's data back in to Henry.

We set one up on the very top of Brake Hill and another one on the floor of the old abandoned quarry out west of Strawberry Lake. The third one we set up on the big stone slab that's used as the throne in the council ring on top of Indian Hill. We had to get permission from the local chapter of the Daughters of Pocahontas to do this, because they always use the place for their meetings, even though they don't own it. The ladies were very nice about it, though, and decided they couldn't stand in the way of science. Besides, none of them could think of any business they had to bring up at that month's meeting, anyway.

We had to balance each instrument very carefully and make sure the main beam with the bob on it was precisely leveled. Then we had to adjust the tension on the recording arm so that it would make a good trace on the graph paper and still not interfere with the free movement of the beam. All of this took a long time; Homer Snodgrass and Mortimer Dalrymple did most of it, because they have a lot of patience and like to work with fussy stuff like dissecting flies and soldering transistors in place, and stuff like that. Freddy and Dinky and I do a lot better on the big things—like hauling rocks and digging and chopping down trees. Freddy always says it's because we think big.

Anyway, we just sat around chewing the fat most of the time while Homer and Mortimer fussed with each seismograph. Then, when they were satisfied the thing would work all right, we went to work and put a pup tent up over each one to protect it from the weather.

Compared to a lot of the other projects Henry had dreamed up for us, this one seemed pretty dull. All we got out of it was sore feet and a sunburn. We'd make the rounds of the seismograph locations each day and bring back three pieces of graph paper with a squiggly line running down the center. It was always late in the day when we got back, and we were usually pretty hot and tired. Meanwhile, Jeff and Henry just bummed around the clubhouse all day, swapping jokes and eating apple pie that Jeff swiped out of his mother's kitchen.

"Oh, Great Mogul! Would you mind telling us just what this is all about?" said Freddy Muldoon one afternoon as he plumped his ample bottom onto an apple crate and mopped the sweat and dirt off his face.

"I don't mind," said Henry indulgently, as he looked up from the graphs he was studying and pushed his glasses up onto his forehead. "That is, if you think you can understand it."

"Let's give it a try," said Freddy, unperturbed.

"Well, those 'squiggly' lines, as you call them, are a record of every movement in the earth's crust around this area for twenty-four hours. With four recording stations we can get a good picture of how strong the tremors are and what direction they're moving."

"So who cares?" said Freddy, fanning himself.

"A lot of people care," said Henry. "Someday we might have a big earthquake in this area. Who knows?"

"Big deal!" said Freddy. "After all the buildings are knocked flat, we'll know what caused it, huh?"

"Don't be a fat fink!" Mortimer Dalrymple chimed in from where he was lying flat on the floor. "Sometimes I think you just don't know what science is all about."

"Oh yeah?" said Freddy.

"Yeah!" said Mortimer.

And that was all that was said about the matter for several days.

But Henry and Jeff did try to keep our interest up by showing us more of what they were finding out from the graph traces we brought in. They had a lot of them pinned up on the clubhouse walls that they intended to exhibit in their science class when school opened again. The prize exhibits were the three sets of traces that showed how violently the recording arms on the seismographs had oscillated back and forth each time a dynamite blast went off on the banks of Lemon Creek, where they were putting in the footings for a new bridge at Cowper Street. The drums that we mounted the graph paper on for each seismograph were rotated at a rate of one inch an hour by a little electric motor run off a battery. Henry pointed out how we could calculate from the traces just what time each blast went off, and how long it took the shock wave to reach each of our recording stations, and how strong it was when it got there.

But Henry was proudest of the traces that he claimed showed the change in earth vibrations when they turned on the reserve dynamos at the power plant late in the afternoons and then shut them off again late in the evening. Henry said anybody could detect a dynamite blast with his ear, but it took a pretty sensitive instrument to detect a dynamo being turned on.

Even Freddy and Dinky showed more interest in the project after that. Freddy has a very active imagination, and he began dreaming up ways that soldiers might use seismographs in combat to tell when tanks were coming, and things like that. Every time he mentioned this Dinky would give him a great big raspberry, but Freddy insisted it really wasn't any different from the way the Indians would put one ear to the ground so they could tell when the cavalry was coming after them.

On Thursday, when we brought the latest data in from the recording stations, we found Henry and Jeff poring over the previous day's tracings, which they had taken down from the wall. Henry grabbed the new sheets out of my hand and spread them out on the table excitedly.

"Look, Jeff! Here it is again!" he cried, running his finger down the ink trace on one of the sheets. We all crowded around the table to see what Henry was so hipped about. He ran his finger across to the time scale marked on the margin. "See! It's the same time, too. It starts about midnight and ends about four o'clock in the morning. What do you make of it?"

Jeff scratched his head and puckered his brow. "I don't know, Henry. It's sure odd. But maybe it's just a coincidence."

"It can't be a coincidence three nights in a row!"

"I don't see nothin' but a squiggly line," said Freddy Muldoon.

"Shut up!" said Mortimer.

What Henry was pointing to was a series of extremely small oscillations of the recording arm that showed up in the ink trace at very irregular intervals in the early hours of the morning. He spread out the sheets for the past three days, and we could all see little peaks that had been recorded in the ink trace during the same hours on each day, Then they stopped, as though somebody had turned something off, and the line was smooth again.

There wasn't any definable pattern to the peaks. They just occurred at random during a four-hour period and

then disappeared.

"This is a real mystery," said Henry, "If these tremors were caused by a piece of machinery—or anything mechanical—you'd think they would come at regular intervals. There'd be some kind of pattern to them. But there's only one thing regular about this caper. It starts at midnight and stops at four in the morning."

"That's real weird!" said Mortimer Dalrymple.

"Maybe it's a drunk staggering home from a bar, and every once in a while he falls flat on his face," said

Freddy Muldoon.

"Stow it, Freddy!" Jeff Crocker warned him. "It wouldn't take him four hours to get home."

"You oughta be on television," sneered Dinky Poore. "You're almost as funny as the commercials."

"How'd you like to work in my dad's service station?" Mortimer jibed at him. "He could use a real gasser like you."

"Okay, you characters," Henry interrupted. "Maybe what Freddy said isn't so stupid. Maybe he put his finger on the key to the whole thing."

"What do you mean?" asked Jeff.

"Whatever is causing these slight tremors is most likely human in origin. That's what I mean," Henry replied. "Whether he knew it or not, Freddy was *thinking* about the problem when he came up with the crack about the drunk. Maybe it would help if some of the rest of us did a little thinking, too."

"Okay! Everybody think for five minutes!" Mortimer ordered in a loud voice.

"What we've got to think about is who would be up at that time of night, and what might he be doing that he couldn't do in the daytime," Henry continued.

"Maybe it's a night watchman," said Dinky Poore.

"Negative!" said Jeff Crocker. "Most night watchmen are pretty quiet."

"What about the garbage collectors?" said Homer Snodgrass. "They're always banging cans around."

"Too early in the morning for them," said Henry. "Besides, they don't do anything earthshaking."

Then everybody lapsed into silence, because Henry

tilted his piano stool back against the wall and was gazing up into the rafters. We all sat down and waited until Henry got through thinking.

When the legs of the piano stool hit the floor again, Henry's eyes had that gleam in them that we all recognized as the birth of an idea. He moved over to the large map of the county tacked on the clubhouse wall.

"I think we can narrow this problem down a bit," he said quietly. "We can't tell from our recordings *what* is causing these tremors. But we can get some clues from them about *where* the vibrations are coming from."

"Good idea, Henry!" Dinky Poore cried, smelling an adventure. "Then we could sneak up on the place and find out what's going on."

"Exactly!" said Henry. "Now let's get to work."

When Henry said "work" he meant brainwork, so Dinky and Freddy and I went fishing, leaving the rest of them to wrestle with the seismograph tracings and Henry's homemade computer.

When we got back to the clubhouse late in the day, we found reams of paper all over the place, and the county map was all marked up with little circles indicating the locations of our seismograph stations and lines converging on the center of town. On the large map of Mammoth Falls on the other wall, Henry had marked a large red circle that covered about a third of the downtown business section.

"We think the source of these tremors is somewhere in this area," he said, tracing the circle with his finger. "Now, here's what we've decided to do." But before he could get started, Jeff Crocker rapped his gavel on the packing crate he uses for a podium, had the door locked and the window shades drawn, and called the club into secret session.

Late that night I sneaked out of the house by shinnying down the drainpipe outside my window and met Dinky and Freddy in the alley back of Dinky's house. It was near midnight, and we made our way downtown through vacant lots and back alleys so nobody would see us and wonder what we were doing out that time of night. I carried a hand transceiver so we could keep in communication with the clubhouse, where Henry and Jeff were monitoring the seismograph. Dinky carried a radiosonde transmitter strapped to the back of his belt that gave out a constant *beep* signal. This would make it possible for Henry and Jeff to know where we were at all times, in case we couldn't talk on the radio. There was a directional antenna on our receiver, at the clubhouse, and Homer and Mortimer had taken another one out to the seismograph station on Indian Hill. Between the two of them they could get a fix on our location at any time.

We sneaked through all the alleys of the downtown section as quietly as we could. Every few feet we would stop and listen carefully and put our hands lightly on the ground to see if we could pick up any kind of vibrations. It was pretty slow going, and Henry would keep calling us on the radio to tell us to move along faster, or switch over to another block. We were groping our way down the narrow, cobblestoned alley behind Jamieson's Variety Store when we heard something that brought us up short. It was a series of dull thuds, spaced about one second apart.

"Jeepers!" said Freddy, and we all froze in place with our eyes and ears alert.

The thudding had stopped, and we waited breathlessly in the darkness. Then it started again. Dinky moved forward very cautiously, with his tousled head thrust forward. He paused for a moment, listening intently, then swung his arm in a wide arc motioning us toward the angle in the back wall of Jamieson's where the elevator shaft jutted out into the alley. We waited there for a few moments in the deep shadow of the wall. It was so quiet you could hear the sweat from Freddy's forehead dripping onto the cobblestones.

When the thudding noises started again Dinky inched his way around the corner of the elevator wall, and we followed. Just then Henry called on the radio. "This is High Mogul," he said. I cupped my hand around the mouthpiece of the transceiver and said, "Shut up!" in a hoarse whisper and shut the thing off. We crept along the wall of the elevator shaft and rounded the second corner to where it joined the wall of the main building again. There was a thin sliver of light visible at the corner of one of the basement windows.

"Holy mackerel!" said Freddy Muldoon.

"There must be someone down there," Dinky whispered, with his hand cupped around my ear. "What'll we do now?"

"We can't back out now!" I whispered back. "Let's go for broke!"

Dinky nodded. "Wait 'til the noise starts again." When the pounding commenced once more, Dinky got down on all fours and crept up to the basement window. A gunnysack had been tacked over it, but the sliver of light we had seen came from the left edge of the window where the burlap had curled back. Dinky pressed one eye up close to the window jamb and peered in. When he pulled his head back he was waving frantically at me. I crawled up beside him and peeked inside.

There were four men in the basement. One of them was holding a kerosene lantern in his hand at shoulder height. Another was sitting on a packing crate, smoking a cigarette. The other two were working at a gaping hole in one wall with a sledge hammer and a crowbar padded with burlap. I pulled my head back and I looked along the alley to re-orient myself. I was right! The building right next to Jamieson's was the Mammoth Falls Trust and Deposit Company.

I looked at Dinky, and he looked at me. Just then the pounding stopped. We both pressed our eyes up to the window. The man with the cigarette had gotten up off the packing crate and moved to the wall. He took three oblong objects the color of butter from a wooden box and crammed them into the farthest recess of the hole in the wall. He must have had to go in quite a way, because he reached in all the way up to his waist. When he pulled himself out, the other men went to work and tamped a lot of loose rubble back into the hole and fixed it in place with some cement. Then they all sat down and lighted cigarettes.

We waited breathlessly in the darkness. When nothing had happened after a minute or two, I crept back around the wall of the elevator shaft and tried to reach Henry on the radio. I had just gotten him to answer when there was a muffled explosion. I could feel the wall of the elevator shaft tremble a bit. The seat of my pants seemed to rise an inch or so off the cobblestones, and I sat back down again, hard.

"What on earth was that?" Henry shouted into the radio. "The needle on the graph just jumped a mile!"

"I think it was an explosion," I gulped. "There are some men in Jamieson's basement, and they've been digging through the wall into the bank!"

"Go get the police!" Henry shouted. "We'll try to call them from Jeff's house."

I started back around the wall of the elevator shaft to get Freddy and Dinky, and stopped just in time. The figure of a big, burly man loomed out of the shadows. He grabbed both of them by the collar while they were still peering through the slit in the window.

"Lemme go, you big moose!" Freddy shouted, struggling to get free.

"Shut up, Fatso, or I'll bash your head against the wall!" the man muttered in a gruff voice.

I didn't wait to hear any more. I crept back around the corner and then darted down the alley, heading for the police station. A car was backing slowly up the alley with no lights on. The driver slapped his brakes on when he saw me flash past, and I heard his door swing open. But I didn't wait to answer any questions. I just kept running and slid around the corner into Walnut Street. I could hear footsteps pounding behind me, but by the time they reached the head of the alley I was already half a block up the street, and whoever was chasing me turned around and went back.

The next fifteen minutes seemed like one of those nightmares you have when you're trying to holler for help and no sound comes out of your mouth. All I could think about was Dinky and Freddy struggling with that big brute in the alley, and I must have sprinted the six blocks to the police station in 10 seconds flat.

But when I got there the door was locked and there was just one feeble light burning in a goose-necked lamp on the night desk. I could see Constable Billy Dahr's feet propped up on the desk, but his head was out of sight in the shadows.

I rattled the door and pounded on it with my fists and hollered like bloody blazes, but his feet didn't even move. I could hear the phone ringing and knew it must be Jeff and Henry calling in, but Billy Dahr was snoring too loud to even hear it. Finally I dashed around to a side window and threw a big rock through it. You'd have thought Armageddon had come. Billy Dahr bolted up out of the swivel chair, like a punch-drunk fighter answering the bell, and sent the goose-necked lamp flying onto the floor. The office was plunged into darkness. I could hear him cursing and stumbling around inside, trying to find the light switch.

When he had finally gotten the lights on and unlocked the front door for me, I knew I'd have a lot explaining to do. I decided not to answer any questions.

"Call Chief Putney, quick!" I shouted, before Billy Dahr could open his mouth. "Some men are trying to rob the bank!"

"What in tarnation?" Billy muttered, rubbing his eyes. "Is them the ones threw that rock through the window?"

"Forget the rock, Constable Dahr," I said, pushing him back through the door. "I had to throw it to wake you up. Please call the chief right away. Freddy and Dinky are back there in the alley and—"

Billy Dahr was rummaging through the drawers of the desk. I picked up the phone and handed it to him. "Here's the phone. Call him, quick!"

"That there ain't no help," mumbled Billy, pushing the phone back down on the desk. "I don't know his number. Now where's that danged phone book?" and he went on rummaging through the desk.

I finally picked up the phone myself and dialed the operator.

"Get me the police," I said. "It's an emergency!"

I could hear her dialing, and then she came back on the line and said she was sorry but the number was busy.

"Please keep trying, operator; it's urgent!"

"Okay!" she said. "I'll keep trying and call you right back. Where are you calling from?"

"From the police station," I said.

There was a pause. Then she said, "Maybe that's why the number is busy."

"I'm sorry, operator," I apologized. "I want Chief Putney's home."

"Do you have the number?"

"No!"

"I'll connect you with Information."

And that's the way things went. By the time we got Chief Putney out of bed and pulled up in the alley back of Jamieson's with a squad car, the place was quiet as a tomb and there was no sign of Dinky and Freddy.

"I'll betcha they've been kidnapped!" I cried.

"Now take it easy, son," said Chief Putney in his slow, methodical voice. "Let's not jump to conclusions."

Two policemen clambered into the basement of Jamieson's and came back to report that there was a hole big enough for a man to crawl through right into the vault of the Mammoth Falls Trust and Deposit Company.

"The vault's been pretty well cleaned out," one of them said. "No telling how much they got away with!"

"If that don't beat all!" said Billy Dahr.

It was then I remembered that I hadn't told Henry and Jeff what had happened. When I switched on the radio, Jeff had been trying to reach me and he sounded like a fishwife.

"Where on earth have you been for the last fifteen minutes? And what are you doing way out there west of town?"

"I'm not way out west of town," I said. "I'm right here in the alley back of the bank."

"Well what's going on? We're getting beeps from the radiosonde way out on White Fork Road. It's been moving west for the last ten minutes."

"That's Dinky and Freddy," I said. "I think they've been kidnapped!"

"Kidnapped? Cut the comedy, Charlie. What's going on?"

"Honest Injun, Jeff!" And I told him about the big man grabbing Dinky and Freddy, and about the car backing up into the alley.

"Is Chief Putney there?" Jeff asked. I told him he

was. "Tell him we've got a fix on where that transmitter is. And if it's still on Dinky's belt, and Dinky's been kidnapped, then we know where the bank robbers are."

I climbed down into Jamieson's basement and collared Chief Putney and told him what Jeff had told me. At first he didn't seem to understand.

"Why don't you kids mind your own business and stop interfering!" he growled. "You ought to be home in bed, anyway." But then Billy Dahr reminded him that if it hadn't been for me running to the police station they wouldn't even have known the bank had been robbed.

"I guess you're right, Billy," said the chief. "But I never saw such a nosey bunch of kids in all my life. Some day I'm going to find out how they always seem to be around when things go wrong."

"Henry says if you'll send a squad car up to Jeff Crocker's barn he can tell them where the transmitter signals are coming from. Then you can put it out on the police net."

"Okay! Okay!" said Chief Putney, clapping one hand to his forehead. "Maybe your friend Henry would like to run the whole operation."

"We're just trying to help out," I told him.

Chief Putney got on the radio and sent a squad car from the county sheriff's office to Jeff Crocker's barn. Then he alerted the state highway patrol and asked them to set up roadblocks in a wide circle around Mammoth Falls.

"What about the FBI?" I asked him. "This is a kidnap case."

"Please go lie down someplace, Charlie!" the chief groaned. "I don't want to have to arrest myself for child-beating."

Just then a squad car from the sheriff's office pulled into the alley with its beacon light flashing and its siren screaming. An officer stuck his head out of the window.

"Just got a call from the control car," he said. "They say that car isn't moving west any more. It's stopped up in the hills west of Strawberry Lake. How on earth can they tell where that car is?"

"Black magic!" said Chief Putney. "I just caught one of the magicians."

"Who? That kid over there?"

"Yeah! Put him in your car so we know where he is. If you get a chance, have someone phone his parents so they know he's all right. Let's get going!"

The chief's car screamed off into the darkness, heading toward the White Fork Road. My head snapped back against the cushion of the rear seat of the sheriff's car as we took off after it. Two of Chief Putney's men stayed behind to guard the bank vault.

Meanwhile, Dinky and Freddy found themselves being bound and gagged and thrust through the door of a log cabin in the hills overlooking Strawberry Lake. They had both been blindfolded back in the alley, so they didn't know where they had been taken or what for. But they knew the car had been climbing a winding road for some time, and Dinky could smell the odor of gun oil and kerosene. He guessed they might be in one of the small hunting lodges that dotted the area around the old zinc mine and the limestone quarry. The two men who pushed them through the door followed inside and tied them securely to the end posts of a double bunk against one wall of the cabin. As the door was closing behind them, Dinky drove one elbow into Freddy's ribs.

"Ouch!" yelped Freddy.

"I'm glad they didn't steal my transistor radio," said Dinky, in a hoarse whisper.

"What's that about a radio?" said the big, hulking man, kicking open the door again.

"It's just an old radio," said Dinky. "It belongs to my little sister."

"I seen something on the back of that kid's belt when we pushed him through the door," said the other man.

"I think we'll just take it," said the big man. "It might come in handy."

"Please don't take it! My sister doesn't know I have it," cried Dinky, squirming to press his back against the bunk post.

"Now ain't that just too bad!" said the gruff voice of the big man, as he whipped Dinky's belt from his trousers. "Maybe that'll teach ya to mind your own business after this."

The big man thrust the transmitter into one of the money bags taken from the bank vault, and the two slipped out the door, slamming it closed behind them.

"You some kind of a nut?" asked Freddy, in a terse whisper. "Now nobody will ever find us."

"They might find the money, though. And the robbers, too." Dinky snickered.

They heard the car start again outside. It passed right behind the cabin, went a short distance, and then the sound of the engine stopped.

"Maybe they're out of gas," said Freddy.

"I don't think so," said Dinky. "Listen a minute."

Suddenly they heard the sound of branches breaking, followed by a tremendous crash, more branches breaking, and the clanking and ringing sound of metal striking stone.

"Holy mackerel!" They must have driven over a cliff!" cried Freddy.

"Shut up!" warned Dinky, digging him again in the ribs. "They'll be back here again. All they did was shove the car down the side of the hill."

"What for? Are they nuts, or somethin'?"

"Don't you ever watch TV?" sneered Dinky. "Robbers always get rid of the getaway car. That's the one the police would be looking for."

"What are they gonna do? Walk?"

"No! They probably have another car stashed away in the woods somewhere."

Dinky and Freddy waited breathlessly for further sounds from outside the cabin, but the minutes ticked past and not a sound broke the stillness of the woods.

But the steady *beep-beep-beep* of the telltale transmitter could be heard clearly by Henry and Jeff back in the Crockers' barn, as it swung to and fro in the canvas bag carried by one of the bank robbers. It was moving so slowly now that the directional finders could barely detect its progress. Henry showed the sheriff's deputies at the barn the spot on the map where he thought the beeps were coming from. They seemed to be moving toward the old abandoned zinc mine.

"Maybe they figure on hiding out in the mine until the heat's off," said Jeff.

"If they do, they've got a surprise coming!" said one of the deputies, and he went out to his car to get Chief Putney on the radio.

By this time, Dinky had managed to wriggle free from the ropes that bound him to the bunk post. Very quietly, he started to untie Freddy.

"How'd you do it?" asked Freddy, in a whisper. "My wrists are so stiff I can't move 'em."

"It's a cinch!" said Dinky. "When somebody ties you up, just tense all your muscles and keep 'em as tight as you can. When you relax, the ropes are loose and you can get out, if you're good."

"Where'd you learn that?"

"I read it in a book about Houdini!"

"About who did what?"

"About Houdini. That's a man's name."

"Oh! One of them sneaky Indians, huh?"

"No! He was just a plain old American and a real cool magician."

"Okay! Whatta we do now?" asked Freddy.

"Well, we don't have any radio, and it's too far to walk back to town, so we're gonna start a great big bonfire outside and let people know where we are."

"What about the robbers?" asked Freddy. "Won't they see the fire and come back and clobber us?"

"I don't think so," said Dinky. "They gotta keep making tracks and clear out of here. They don't have time to come back now."

"How we gonna start a fire? We don't have any matches."

"I've got a knife," said Dinky. "That's all we need."

"Okay, Mac! Make with the knife!" said Freddy. "Is this some more of your Houdini stuff?"

"No," Dinky said offhandedly. "This is a sneaky old Indian trick."

Dinky really is a whiz with a knife. In no time at all he had cut a good springy bow from a small birch branch and stripped a long piece of bark from a root to make a thong for it. Then he whittled a small hole in a flat piece of wood he found in the cabin and carved out a blunt-ended drill about the size of a tent peg from a piece of pine. He had Freddy strip some dry shreds of tinder from the inside of the bark on an old log lying in back of the cabin, and he was ready to start a fire.

"C'mon, magician, let's make with the heat!" said Freddy, jumping up and down. "I'm cold." For all his blubber, Freddy gets cold quicker than anybody else in our gang. And his teeth were chattering now, from sitting on the cold cabin floor.

Dinky knelt on the ground with one foot on the flat board and twisted the thong of the bow around the pine drill. Then he inserted the blunt end of the drill in the little hole he'd made in the board and started to rotate it rapidly back and forth, making long, sawing motions with the bow, like a bass fiddle player. Freddy watched in amazement as the end of the drill got hot and began to smoke. Pretty soon he could smell the odor of burning pine. Then, suddenly, Dinky sprang to his feet and popped a hot spark from the board into a handful of the dry tinder. He started dancing around in a circle with it, waving it in the wind and blowing on it. The smoke from the tinder got thicker and thicker, and then it suddenly burst into flame.

"How! How!" cried Dinky, in real Indian fashion. "Ouch!" he yelped, as the flaming tinder burnt his hand.

He dropped the burning mass into a pile of dry leaves, and he and Freddy sprinkled wood shavings and twigs on it until they had a good blaze going. Then they built a crib of larger logs around the fire and soon had a raging inferno that threw a column of flame thirty feet into the air.

You could see the light from the fire all the way back to Mammoth Falls. The sheriff's deputy outside Jeff Crocker's barn saw it and called Chief Putney's car on the radio.

"Looks like a big fire up in the hills right where you're heading. Can you see it?"

"Negative!" Chief Putney called back. "We're in the woods. Can't see anything."

"The kid inside says it might be one of those hunting lodges up there. Better check it out. He says he's still getting radio signals pretty steady from around the old zinc mine."

Just then the car I was riding in shot around a sharp bend in the road, and out of the corner of my eye I caught a flash of light from among the trees over on the next ridge of hills. I pounded the driver on the shoulder and shouted to him to stop.

"We're on the wrong road," I told him. "I just saw a flash of light through the trees, and it came from those hills on the other side of the creek."

The driver slammed on his brakes. "How do we get there?"

"Go back to the wooden bridge," I told him. "There's an old logging road that goes up to that ridge."

The deputy called Chief Putney on the radio while we backed around in a clearing. Soon we were climbing through the trees up the slopes of the other ridge, with the chief's car following us. The sheriff's deputy was really gunning it up the twisting, deeply rutted road, and I was tossing around in the back seat like a sack of potatoes, trying to find something to hold onto.

The chief's voice came over the radio. "Don't run your siren! And dim your lights when we get near the top!" he said. "If the men we're looking for are up there, we want to surprise them."

But when we rounded the last hairpin turn and pulled into the brightly lighted clearing where the fire was raging, all we could see were the figures of Dinky and Freddy, dancing like two wild Indians silhouetted against the flames.

"The robbers took off into the woods!" shouted Freddy. "They pushed their car down the hill over there."

"How long ago?" asked the chief.

"Maybe twenty minutes, maybe more," said Dinky. "Bet they got another car stashed away somewhere."

"If they have, they'd have to come back down this road with it," said the sheriff's deputy. "There isn't any other road leading off this ridge, is there?"

"Not that I know of," I told him. "This is the only one."

"Then they must be planning on hiding out somewhere until the heat's off. The last report on the net said those radio beeps were coming from up near the old zinc mine."

"I can't figure it out," said Chief Putney. "If they plan to hide out here in the hills, *why* did they leave these two kids behind to give us a lead on where they were? If they hole up in the mine it might take us a week to smoke 'em out, but all we have to do is blockade the entrance and they're stuck! I just can't figure it out."

"It almost seems like they *wanted* us to follow them," said the deputy.

Suddenly a thought struck me. "Wait a minute!" I cried, grabbing the chief's arm. "There *is* another road off this ridge. Only it isn't an automobile road; it's a railroad. It's the old branch line running up to Hyattsville from the zinc mine. You know the one, Chief. It crosses Turkey Hill Road right at The Gap."

"That's the third nutty thing you've said tonight!" said the chief. "I suppose they have the California Zephyr waiting there to take them to San Francisco!"

"I don't know about the California Zephyr," I said, "but they could use old Leapin' Lena. That's that old handcar that's parked in the loading yard. It works, too!"

"Maybe the kid's right, Chief," said the sheriff's deputy. "Maybe they hoped we *would* follow them on foot—and get stuck up there by the mine with no radio while they made a getaway down the railroad. It's downhill all the way to Hyattsville. They could make thirty miles an hour easy with that rusty handcar and never come near one of our roadblocks."

Just then the radio in the squad car started squawking. It was Henry, wanting to talk to Chief Putney.

"We've still got a fix on that transmitter," he said in a shrill voice, "and it's started moving straight north. Pretty fast, too. We figure they're following that old railroad spur from the zinc mine. They're probably heading for Hyattsville."

"You ain't telling me nothing I don't already know!" said the chief haughtily. "We already figured that out."

"Oh!" said Henry.

"And by the way," said the chief, "we found your two partners in crime and they're all right. So you can tell their folks to pick 'em up at the station in the morning."

"You mean they're under arrest? But we didn't do anything, Chief!"

"Let's just say I have them in protective custody."

"What does that mean?"

"It means I'm not letting any of you kids out of my sight until we've nabbed those bank bandits."

"How are you going to do that unless I tell you where they are?" said Henry. "They've already figured out how to get through all your roadblocks."

"You can only go one place on a railroad, sonny. We'll be waiting for them at the end of the line."

"What if they get off before the end of the line?"

"You're full of bright ideas!" said the chief. "Do you

think they're stupid enough to take off on foot again?"

"No!" said Henry. "I think they planned their getaway better than that."

"Well, if they've got another car waiting where that track passes under the state highway, we'll catch 'em in one of our roadblocks."

"They've already passed the state highway," said Henry, "and our tracking antennas tell us they're still heading toward Hyattsville."

"Good! Then we'll get 'em at the end of the line."

"You're not thinking, Chief."

"See here, young Mulligan, I'll—"

"Haven't you ever dreamed about what you'd do if you were a bank robber?"

"No, I haven't!" fumed the chief.

"Well, I have," said Henry. "And I'll bet one of our dinosaur eggs that I know just what they're planning."

"Is that so? Well, supposing you tell me."

"What about Dinky and Freddy?"

"Okay! Okay! We'll see they get home all right," said the chief. "Now, tell me your brilliant idea."

"Well, if I were a bank robber I think I'd have a boat waiting at the railroad trestle over Lemon Creek. And with good luck I'd probably be out into the lakes and all the way to Canada before you figured out what happened."

There was a long silence.

"Are you still there, Chief?" asked Henry, finally. "Do you want me to phone Mr. Monaghan's boathouse? You could probably nab them at the mouth of Lemon Creek if you get a couple of patrol cars down there right away."

Chief Putney was fuming and sputtering.

"You're a crazy nut, Mulligan!" he said at last. "Now, suppose you get off the radio and let me be the Chief of Police."

"Okay! Okay!" said Henry. "I was just trying to help."

"That's the kind of help I can do without," said the chief. "Now get off the air and let me talk to Officer Riley."

"This is Riley, Chief," came a new voice.

"Listen, Riley, turn your volume down," whispered the chief. "Now, is that kid still around?"

"No, Chief. He went back in the barn."

"Good! Now listen, Riley. I want you to get two cars down to Monaghan's boathouse at the river right away. Call him on the phone and tell him to get a couple of boats ready. I think those crooks might try to make a getaway down Lemon Creek."

"Good thinking, Chief! What about these kids?"

"Riley, I think we can play cops and robbers without having those kids underfoot. Leave 'em there in the barn."

"I just thought that direction finder of theirs might come in handy."

"You're not being paid to think! Just follow orders."

"Right, Chief!"

"See that these kids all get home right away," Chief Putney said to the sheriff's deputy. "Then report to the control center at Crocker's barn. I'm heading for Monaghan's boathouse." The chief's car showered us with gravel as the driver spun it around and headed

pell-mell down the road.

The deputy helped us throw dirt over the remains of the bonfire, and then Dinky and Freddy and I clambered into his car.

"I hope the Chief's doing the right thing," he said, as he nursed the car down the road off the ridge. "It might not be so easy spotting that boat in the dark. I've been duck hunting in those bulrushes at the mouth of the creek and they spread out pretty far. There's a lot of places a boat could slip through without ever getting near Monaghan's boathouse."

"They wouldn't get away if Henry were there with our direction finder," I said.

"You got a portable set?"

"Sure! We have a battery power pack, and we can take it anywhere."

The deputy looked at his watch and rubbed his chin. Then there was a long silence. Suddenly, when we reached the hardtop of the county road, he flicked on his flashing beacon and the tires screamed as he pushed the accelerator to the floor.

"This'll be the first time in my life I didn't follow orders," he said.

We must have waked up all of Jeff Crocker's family when we skidded into the driveway beside the barn. The deputy turned the car around while I rushed in and got Henry.

"They're heading down Lemon Creek, all right—as close as we can figure," said Henry, as we piled into the deputy's car with the battery set. "Jeff'll keep a track on them and let us know if there's any change."

"Hey! What's going on, Sergeant?" a policeman shouted from the control car parked beside the barn.

"Just call me 'Corporal'!" the deputy hollered back. "See you in court!" And we spun out of the driveway with the siren wide open.

The deputy kept glancing at his watch as we sped down the state highway toward the turnoff for the river. Henry had turned our receiver on and was holding it up to the window of the car, trying to pick up the signal of the telltale transmitter. There was nothing coming over the police net.

"I hope we get there in time," said the deputy. "The Chief had about ten minutes start on us and he didn't have to drive as far."

"Don't worry," said Henry. "Jeff is telephoning Mr. Monaghan. He'll have another boat ready for us."

"How'm I gonna explain this to Chief Putney?" moaned the deputy, clapping one hand to his forehead.

"Maybe you won't have to," cried Henry. "I think I've got something! Pull over! Pull over to the side of the road!"

The deputy braked the car down sharply, and we ground to a halt on the apron. "What's the matter? What's up?" he asked, twisting round in his seat.

Henry turned his loop antenna a hair to the right and turned the volume up on the speaker. Then he took his earphones off. The steady *beep-beep-beep* of Dinky's little transmitter was clearly audible.

"Have you got a map?" Henry asked the deputy.

"Sure!" He reached in the glove compartment, pulled out a road map, and spread it on the seat beside him.

"Where are we right now?" asked Henry, shining his flashlight on the map.

"I'd say we were right about here." The deputy pointed to a jog in the red line marking the state highway.

Henry pulled his compass from his pocket and took a reading in the direction the antenna was pointing. Then he marked an "X" on the map where Lemon Creek took a sharp turn toward the river.

"I figure they're just about there, now. They've got at least three miles to go before they reach the river."

"That ought to take them twenty or twenty-five minutes," said the deputy. "I'm sure they're using a rowboat or a canoe."

"They must be," I said. "A motorboat would make too much noise."

"Let's get going!" Henry urged. "We won't go to Monaghan's boathouse. Turn right, down the Old Mill Road."

"The Old Mill Road? Are you nuts?"

"Please, Officer!" Henry pleaded. "We've only got about ten minutes."

"Oh, boy!" said the deputy. "You're going to get me in real trouble!"

"You're in trouble already," said Henry. "How would you like a chance to be a hero?"

"A live hero or a dead hero?"

"How would you like to capture those bank bandits single-handed?" Henry persisted.

"Sonny, I hear you talking, but I've got a wife and kids to think about."

"They'll be proud of you after tonight," said Henry. "Let's get going!"

"Oh, boy! I should have taken you kids home, like the chief told me!" mumbled the deputy, as he put the car in gear and pulled it onto the highway.

As we turned down the road leading to the old abandoned mill on Lemon Creek, Henry outlined his plan.

"It's simple," he said. "They ought to reach the millpond in about ten minutes. The only way to get out of it is to go through the sluiceway. That's a natural trap. If we can close the downstream gate before they get there, we'll have them blocked. And if we close the upstream gate after they're in the sluice, they can't possibly get out. The walls are about fifteen feet high and covered with green slime. They'll be helpless! All we have to do is sit there and wait for the chief to come."

Even the deputy was smiling now, and he pushed the patrol car down the winding road even faster than before. "Great idea, Mulligan! Great!" he exclaimed. Then he frowned. "But what about those gates? Will they work?"

"Sure they will," I said. "The sluice is still used as a lock to let boats out of the millpond. The winches are still in good shape. We've closed the gates lots of times to trap fish."

"Remind me to tell the game warden about that," said the deputy.

"Forget it!" said Freddy Muldoon. "That's just one of Charlie's fish stories."

"Do you have any tear gas?" Henry asked.

"Yeah!" said the deputy. "That's a good idea. There's two grenades in the glove compartment there. Get 'em out."

"Put your lights out before we get to the creek," Henry warned. "We don't want to tip them off."

"Okay, Chief!" said the deputy. "Any other orders?"

The deputy pulled the car off the road about a hundred yards short of the creek, and we ran the rest of the way to the millhouse. With a half moon in the east there was just enough light to see by. The old millhouse is a pretty sneaky place to be messing around in when it's dark, but we knew every nook and cranny of it by heart. Dinky and Freddy clambered across the catwalk to the other side of the sluice and lay flat on their bellies on top of the wall. Henry and I took the deputy into the winch house, and the three of us lowered the downstream gate. It creaked and groaned a lot, but we figured the bank bandits were still far enough away so that they couldn't hear it.

"Don't close it all the way," Henry advised. "We don't want the water level to rise too high in the sluice. After we've shut the upstream gate, we can let it down the rest of the way."

We crawled out onto the milldam and lay there behind the railing holding our breath. The only sound came from the water gurgling under the downstream sluice gate, and we hoped the men we were waiting for weren't smart enough to recognize the sound and realize the gate was closed. Henry had the directional receiver tuned again and was rotating the antenna, trying to get a fix on the transmitter signal. He had just picked up the beep when I could see the dim outline of a small boat ease out of the shadows about two hundred yards upstream and move into a patch of moonlight. I grabbed Henry by the elbow and he shut off the receiver. We crawled back to the winch house, leaving the deputy lying flat on his stomach near the upstream gate.

Inside the winch house we waited, crouched in the darkness, for the signal that would tell us when to close the upstream gate. It seemed like it was forever, and I could hear Henry breathing just as clear as the blower on our hot air furnace at home. I was sweating all over and shaking with chills at the same time. I figured this must be how an eel would feel in a Turkish bath.

Suddenly a flash of light flicked at the window of the

winch house. It was the signal from the deputy that the boat had entered the sluice. Henry and I sprang into action and threw our weight against the trunnion of the winch. My feet slipped from under me and I tripped Henry, and we both fell to the floor, but we managed to spin the winch fast enough to close the upstream gate before the men in the boat knew what was happening. Then we dashed to the other winch and lowered the downstream gate the rest of the way.

When we scrambled out to our places along the guard rail at the edge of the sluice, the boat had already rammed against the downstream gate. There were sounds of confusion and violent cursing coming up from the bottom of the dark chamber in which the bandits were trapped. The bright beam of the deputy's flashlight stabbed into the depths of the sluiceway and came to rest on the figures of four men huddled in a small rowboat. The deputy's voice rang out in a booming command that resonated back and forth between the walls of the sluice.

"Throw your guns in the water! You're surrounded!"

Four more beams of light hit the bandits in the face as Dinky, Freddy, Henry, and I flicked on our flashlights from opposite sides of the sluice. The men in the boat threw their hands up, and one of them shouted, "Don't shoot! Don't shoot! We're just going fishing."

"You can't fish with a rod like that!" the deputy shouted back. "Throw it in the water!"

There was a splash as the pistol dropped from the hand of the man standing in the stern of the boat.

"Get the rest of them overboard before we load your

boat with tear gas!"

Three more weapons splashed in the water. The man in the bow of the boat reached under the seat and tried to slip a canvas sack over the side, but the deputy's pistol cracked like a whip and a bullet nicked the gunwale beside him.

"Leave the money where it is!" barked the deputy. "Put your hands on top of your head and lie down in the boat!"

It isn't easy for one man to lie down in a rowboat, let alone four. But when you have to, you find a way to do it, and the four bank bandits were smart enough to figure it out.

"Okay, Mulligan. Get on the radio and tell 'em it's all over," said the deputy calmly. And Henry made tracks for the patrol car.

"You characters ought to know you can't fish in this county before daybreak," said the deputy, as he lighted a cigarette. "Now, just as soon as we can truck a ladder in here, we'll get you out of there."

It only took about ten minutes for two more patrol cars to show up at the old mill. And we didn't need a ladder to get the captives out of the sluice. We just opened the upper gate long enough to float the boat up to the top of the wall, and the bank robbers climbed out meek as lambs. I don't think they ever knew there was only one policeman on the scene when they threw their guns in the water.

Freddy Muldoon ran up and kicked the biggest man right in the shins. "That's for calling me 'Fatso'!" he shouted, and then he retreated to a safe distance. One of the policemen grabbed him by the collar and half carried him off the dam. The big man stood there with his mouth open, rubbing one leg against the other.

"There ought be a law against kids," he said. "I knew there'd be trouble when I found them two in the alley."

"What about my transmitter?" Dinky asked. "It's in one of those canvas bags."

"We'll have to hold it for evidence, sonny," said one of the policemen. "You'll get it back later on."

Chief Putney didn't get in on the capture. He and three other policemen were blockading the mouth of Lemon Creek with two motorboats, and they didn't have a radio. It wasn't until daybreak that they saw Mr. Monaghan standing at the end of his dock waving a pair of red flannel drawers at them. When they got back to the police station we were all sitting around sipping hot chocolate and talking to a reporter from the Mammoth Falls *Gazette*. Henry asked Chief Putney if he could send a patrol car out to Indian Hill to pick up Homer and Mortimer.

"You've just given me a great idea," grumbled the chief. "We don't need a police department around here any more. What we need is a good all-night taxi service. Have you got fifty cents for the fare?"

"No!" said Henry.

"Oh, that's really too bad!" said the chief, sarcastically. Then he turned to Billy Dahr and told him to send a car out to Indian Hill.

The Cool Cavern

The Mad Scientists' Club always has a bunch of projects hanging fire that we hope to do something about someday. For instance, one of Henry Mulligan's favorite ideas has always been to build a submarine that we could use to explore the bottom of Strawberry Lake. Henry has a theory that the lake wasn't always as big as it is now. He figures there might be a lot of interesting Indian relics on the lake bottom, and maybe even a whole Indian village.

The trouble is it takes a lot of know-how and a lot of expensive material to build a submarine, and somehow or other we never quite got started on the project, though Henry and Jeff Crocker drew a lot of interesting plans.

But one day Freddy Muldoon came up with some information that changed the whole picture. Sometimes we call Freddy "Little Bright Eyes"—which is his Indian name—and it isn't just because they're the only part of him that isn't fat. It's because Freddy frequently notices things that escape everyone else's attention. It was he and Dinky, for instance, who really solved the mystery of the money hidden in the old cannon out at Memorial Point when they noticed the strange gold key dangling from the neck of Elmer Pridgin.

The information Freddy came up with was a news item in the Mammoth Falls *Gazette*. Nobody else had noticed it; but Freddy reads the whole paper, line by line, every night, because his father is a linotype operator on the *Gazette*, and Freddy likes to give him the razz-ma-tazz if he finds an error in it.

The item Freddy had noticed was an announcement of a White Elephant Auction being held over in Claiborne for the benefit of the Ladies Auxiliary of the Claiborne General Hospital. Among the "white elephants" donated for the auction was a midget two-man Japanese submarine which the Claiborne American Legion Post had brought back from the Pacific in 1945 as a trophy of war. It had been gathering lots of rust and very few onlookers, ever since, in front of the Legion's meeting hall.

The auction was scheduled for one o'clock Saturday afternoon, so we had to act fast if we wanted to get the thing. Nobody could even guess whether it could still be made to operate, but we all figured we'd just have to gamble on that. If we could get it cheap enough, and the hull was good, Henry claimed we could eventually fit it out with all the gear it needed to make it run again.

"Let's go where the auction is!" quipped Mortimer Dalrymple, trying to keep a straight face.

"Get a load of the comic," said Freddy Muldoon disdainfully, with the closest thing to a sneer his pudgy face could manage.

Jeff Crocker rapped his gavel on the packing crate he uses for a podium.

"How much money have we got in the treasury, Homer?"

"Three dollars and eighty-five cents!" Homer Snodgrass reported without hesitation.

"Are you sure?" asked Jeff, incredulously.

"Three dollars and eighty-five cents," repeated Homer.

There was a lot of discussion about this, and Homer kept insisting that we'd all forgotten about the seven dollars we'd spent on flowers for Constable Billy Dahr when he was in the hospital for two weeks after stepping in a bear trap out by Turkey Run Ridge. Finally Mortimer moved that we call for a count of the cash box, and Homer pulled himself wearily out of his chair.

"I don't know whether I've got the strength for this treasurer's job any more," he groaned. "Excuse me, Mr. President," he said, as he climbed up onto the packing crate in front of Jeff. We all sat there in silence while Homer reached up and flipped a switch on the light cord dangling just above Jeff's head. Then he climbed

down off the packing crate and walked over to the corner of the barn, where we keep our safe. He spun the dial quickly and opened the heavy door. Then he reached inside and brought out a little remote control box for a TV set.

"Wait a minute!" Jeff cried. "Charlie and Dinky, get the window shades."

Dinky and I pulled the shades down on all four windows and Mortimer put the crossbar up to barricade the door. Then Homer pointed the remote control box at the peak of the barn roof and pressed one of the buttons. The rope ladder coiled at the peak of the roof popped open and the weighted end of it plopped to the floor. Homer walked over and climbed slowly up it until he had reached the huge crossbeam that buttresses the roof just over the packing crate. He flung himself over the beam and shinnied along it to the point where it joined with one of the roof stringers. There he flipped another switch and our cash box, dangling on the end of a fine steel cable, was lowered gently to the top of the packing crate in front of Jeff. Jeff got up and walked to the safe, drew the cash box key from it, and held it up for everyone to see. Then he returned to his chair, turned the key in the lock of the cash box, and looked up at Homer.

"Okay!" he said.

Homer pointed the remote control box in his direction and pressed the other button. The lid of the cash box flipped open. Jeff dumped the contents out in front of him and methodically counted the money while the rest of us sat there with our arms and legs crossed and repeated the count after him.

"Three dollars and eighty-seven cents," he announced. "Homer was pretty near right."

"I am right!" came Homer's voice from the rafters. "We never count those two Indian-head pennies. That's our reserve for bad debts."

"Okay, Okay!" said Jeff. "The matter is closed." He put the money back in the cash box and signaled Homer to raise it again to the roof.

"Can I come down now, Mr. President?" asked Homer.

"Yes!" said Jeff.

Despite our shortage of funds we all agreed that we should make the trip to Claiborne to attend the White Elephant Auction. If we couldn't manage to buy the Japanese submarine, at least we could find out who did get it.

"I move that we take all our money with us and let me handle the bidding," said Freddy Muldoon, standing up on his chair to give himself a little better position to argue from.

"That's a great idea!" Mortimer Dalrymple cut in, with his usual sarcasm. "You're a born loser, so we won't have to argue about how much money we have any more."

"Okay, Mr. Bigmouth," Freddy shot back. "Maybe I'm not the world's best horse trader, but at least I know a jackass when I see one."

Mortimer came up out of his chair like a whirling dervish, and Henry and I grabbed him just in time to prevent mayhem. Freddy stood fast, with his hands on his hips and that sneering look on his face again, while Jeff rapped his gavel on the crate. When the commotion had died down, little Dinky Poore stood up, at his most truculent, and said, "Mr. President, I second the motion, whether anybody likes it or not!"

In the Mad Scientists' Club, when anybody seconds a motion it's almost sure to pass. The reason is that Freddy and Dinky vote in favor of almost everything, and Jeff Crocker, the president, only votes in case of a tie. So anybody making a motion knows that he has three votes to start with. And if somebody is dumb enough to second his motion, he knows that he's got it made because four votes are already in the bag. But if Freddy or Dinky makes the motion, it's a little different of course. You might say that they face an uphill fight.

In this case, I felt a little sorry for Freddy, so I voted in favor of letting him handle the bidding for the submarine. After Henry and Homer and Mortimer had all voted "no," it was up to Jeff Crocker to decide the issue. He flipped a coin and it came down "heads" and he figured that was a good omen. So he voted in favor of Freddy risking our three dollars and eighty-five cents.

By ten o'clock Saturday morning we were all piled into Zeke Boniface's wheezing old junk truck, Richard the Deep Breather, jolting along on the seventy-five-mile drive to Claiborne. Dinky and Freddy were crouched down behind the seat of the open cab, playing mumblety-peg on the wooden truck bed and exchanging conspiratorial whispers. The rest of us didn't pay too much attention to them. We were too busy figuring out how we would load the submarine on the truck and haul it back to Mammoth Falls, if we were lucky enough to get it. We had brought along the overhead traveling crane rig that Zeke uses to lift engines out of cars, but we were only guessing at how big the sub was, based on Henry's research.

Mortimer Dalrymple had insisted on rigging a hammock between the two chain slings of the traveling crane so he could be comfortable during the trip. Mortimer likes his sleep, and he can catnap right through a club meeting or a dogfight, take your pick. But he didn't get too much sleep on the way to Claiborne. We had the crane stanchion lashed down securely to the truck bed so he wasn't in any danger; but he took some pretty violent lurches (Henry called them "yawing moments") when Zeke threw Richard the Deep Breather into fast-breaking curves on the Claiborne Road. When we pulled into Claiborne Mortimer was pretty seasick; but he'd be the last one to admit it, and the rest of us wouldn't embarrass him by noticing it unless there was some real fun in it. At least he'd escaped the bumps and jolts that the rest of us had to suffer.

The White Elephant Auction was being held in front of the American Legion Hall, because the submarine was the biggest thing on the list and the Legion didn't want to bother moving it off its concrete pedestal unless they were sure it was sold. When Zeke wheeled Richard the Deep Breather into the parking lot there was already a crowd of two or three hundred people gathered in front of the place. The auctioneer was having lunch at a hot dog stand and just marking time until the appointed hour for the auction to begin. We were a little dismayed to see the size of the crowd, but the auctioneer was licking the mustard off his lips with double relish, knowing he had a good thing going.

After we had something to eat we mingled in the crowd and left matters in the hands of Freddy and Dinky, who had all our money. We saw them whispering to each other on the edge of the crowd, and then Freddy got down on all fours and crawled through people's legs up to the front. He ended up to the right of the auctioneer's stand, and Dinky popped up in front of the crowd on the left. A whole bunch of worthless junk was sold at ridiculous prices before the auctioneer got around to mentioning the submarine. It was already three o'clock and Freddy had pulled the last hot dog out of his pocket and eaten it, and was looking around for something to drink, when the auctioneer climbed down off his stand and rapped his gavel on the hull of the sub.

"Ladies and gennemun!" he cried. "Here is the *piece de resistance* of the afternoon. What am I offered for this *genuwine* trophy of war brought back from the far Pacific by the valiant sons of Post 1142 of the American Legion? This is a real conversation piece. Ladies: if you have a real handyman around the house, he can convert this historic tub into the most unique outdoor barbecue you have ever seen. With this symbol of America's triumph over the forces of evil in World War II installed in your backyard, you will be the envy of your neighborhood. Other women will pull out their hair competing for invitations to your evening soirees."

"Blah, blah, blah, blah," said Mortimer. "How about getting down to business?"

Finally the auctioneer pounded his gavel on the rusting hull again and rasped, "What am I offered?"

"Five dollars!" came a squeak from the right side of the semicircle of onlookers. All eyes turned to where Freddy Muldoon stood, looking as nonchalant as his pudgy frame would allow, with one foot crossed over the other and his arms folded in front of him.

"Has he gone nuts?" Mortimer gulped. "That's more money than we have."

"Maybe the truck ride affected his brain," Homer offered. "We'd better go pull him out of there."

"Leave him alone!" Jeff snapped. "We all promised to let him handle this."

The auctioneer paused in mid-sentence. "What was that, my young friend?"

"Five dollars!" Freddy repeated.

The auctioneer snickered indulgently. "Did you hear that, ladies and gennemun?" He laughed. "We have one of the last of the big spenders with us here today—one of America's great natural comedians—and he offers a paltry five dollars for this priceless relic of the late great war." He beat a tattoo on the steel hull of the submarine with his gavel. "Ladies and gennemun!" he cried in a loud voice, raising his hands high in the air and blowing all his words out through his nose. "Ladies and gennemun, I tell you what I'm gonna do. I ordinarily would treat such an offer with the disdain that it deserves. But I can go along with a gag as well as the next one. And just to indulge our young friend here—whom I am sure must be the grandson of the late, great Oliver Hardy—I will open the bidding for five dollars!" Again the gavel descended upon the rusty hull, which was still ringing from the last blow. "Do I hear ten dollars?"

"Four-fifty!" came an even squeakier voice from the left of the crowd.

The auctioneer's jaw dropped. "What was that?" he asked, incredulously.

"I bid four dollars and fifty cents!" said Dinky Poore in a slightly louder voice. There was a laugh from the crowd.

The auctioneer snickered condescendingly again. "I must apologize, ladies and gennemun," he said, fixing a baleful glare on Dinky Poore, "but I didn't realize that we were also honored with the presence of the grandson of Stan Laurel. It isn't every day that you find two jokers in the same deck!" Sweeping his hat from his head, he made an elaborate bow in the direction of Dinky. "Are you aware, young man, that I already have a bid of five dollars?"

"That old tub ain't worth five dollars," said Dinky. "I bid four dollars fifty cents."

The auctioneer clapped his hat back onto his head. "Do I hear ten dollars?" he shouted, banging his gavel on the hull again.

"I think he's right!" said Freddy Muldoon. "I bid four dollars, even."

"Wait a minute!" shouted the auctioneer, pointing

his gavel at Freddy. "You can't pull that on me. You already bid five dollars for this item."

"I changed my mind," said Freddy.

"Do I hear seven-fifty?" shouted the auctioneer.

"Make it three and a half and I'll take it!" Dinky shouted back, cupping hands to his mouth to make himself heard above the laughter of the crowd.

"Three dollars, even!" Freddy hollered.

"Two seventy-five!" countered Dinky.

"I'll go two-fifty, and that's my final offer!" Freddy bellowed.

The auctioneer rapped his gavel on the submarine's hull so hard that the head came flying off. "Sold, sold, sold!" he shouted, pointing the broken handle at Freddy Muldoon. "Sold for two dollars and fifty cents before you can open your big mouth again!"

"I'll take it!" said Freddy. He marched up and put two dollar bills down on the auctioneer's table. Then he turned to Dinky Poore. "Can you lend me fifty cents?"

"Sure!" said Dinky, pulling out a handful of small change; and the crowd roared as he dumped the coins onto the table.

"Get this thing out of here before I change my mind!" fumed the auctioneer.

"Right away, sir!" said Freddy and Dinky.

We needn't have worried about how we were going to load the sub on Zeke's truck. There must have been fifty people from the crowd trying to get a handhold to help us ease it onto the truck bed after we got it suspended in the slings of the traveling crane. We threw a big tarpaulin over it and drove right back to

Mammoth Falls, where we parked it in Zeke's junkyard. We had a lot of work to do on it before we could take it to our hideout, because the first thing we had to do was get it in condition to operate.

Our hideout was made to order for the job we had in mind. It's a real cool cavern hidden from view behind the huge falls where Frenchman's Creek plunges over a precipice about a mile northwest of Strawberry Lake. These are the falls that gave the town its name, and they're a big tourist attraction. But very few people know about the cavern. Almost nobody ever visits it because you have to swim under an overhanging ledge of rock to get to the entrance. Once you get through the narrow opening you're in for a surprise. The cavern widens out into a high-ceilinged chamber with a floor of fine white sand that must have been deposited there when the creek bed was a good deal higher than it is now. The floor of the chamber drops off suddenly after about sixty feet, and there's a deep pool of clear green water dividing the chamber in two. It must be fed by subterranean streams and connected with the lower level of the creek, because the water in it is always the same level as the creek. The place would be a real mecca for sightseers if the town would ever build a covered walkway to the entrance, like they have at Niagara Falls, but they've never had the money.

It's cool as a cucumber inside the cavern, and the temperature stays pretty much the same all year 'round. We use the place as a summer clubhouse sometimes, because it can get pretty hot in Jeff Crocker's barn, and the cavern is a great place to sleep on muggy summer nights. We've fitted it out with a lot of equipment, and we get electricity for free from a generator driven by a waterwheel we installed under the falls. The pool makes a great swimming hole, of course, and we have a first class diving board set up at one end of it. The only problem is we don't get much of a suntan.

While we still had the sub in Zeke's junkyard we took all its running gear apart and cleaned and lubricated all the moving parts. We went over the hull with steel brushes and rust remover and laid on heavy coats of white lead paint. We cut away the net cutter and torpedo guards on the bow with a blowtorch and cut out the torpedo tubes. This gave us a lot of room up front that would have been wasted space. Colonel March at Westport Field helped us get the plexiglass nose section from an old B-17 Flying Fortress in a surplus property sale, and with a little cutting and bending we were able to fit it to the nose of the sub pretty smoothly. When we got finished, she looked pretty sharp with her forty feet of gleaming white hull and her clear plastic nose.

We weren't finished yet, but we decided to move her to the hideout because too many people were snooping around the junkyard to look at her, and we had to throw the tarpaulin over the hull so often that it interfered with our work. Especially, we had to keep an eye peeled for Freddy's cousin Harmon and his gang. They kept turning up at the yard, one or two at a time, pretending to be looking for some piece of junk they knew Zeke didn't have. And one day we saw the whole gang looking at us through field glasses from the edge of a

LADY GODIVE

cliff on Turkey Hill. Actually, they weren't any trouble to us because they couldn't mess around the sub while we were there during the day, and at night we just plain didn't worry about them. Zeke Boniface has a big German shepherd dog named Kaiser Bill, who roams the junkyard all night long. He isn't mean, but he's about one hundred and ten pounds of gleaming white teeth, and he has a way of discouraging people who wander too close to the yard at night.

We named the sub *Lady Go Diver*, which was a name Dinky had suggested, and painted it on both sides of the bow section. On the conning tower we painted the Mad Scientists' Club symbol, which is a test tube crossed over a telescope superimposed on a skull. After we had put new batteries in her and tested the electric motor, we figured we were ready to move her into the cavern under Mammoth Falls to add the finishing touches.

Don't ask me how we got her into the cave. That's our secret. But after we got her in there we could take our time making the rest of the modifications without a lot of people nosing around. Without the torpedo tubes in her she could carry four or five of us easily. We figured on fitting out the bow section as an observer compartment and installing two big searchlights for underwater illumination, one in the bow and one in the conning tower. We also were bargaining with the National Guard Armory down on Vesey Street to get the bulletproof windows out of an old World War II tank they had, so we could install them in the conning tower to give us observation in all directions.

We were getting along pretty well with the work, when one morning we discovered sandy footprints on the hull of the submarine leading to the conning tower. There was sand down inside the controls compartment, too, so we knew somebody had been there. We always cleaned up carefully after finishing work because Henry and Jeff believe in running a taut ship. We checked her over very thoroughly, and as far as we could tell everything was in working order and nothing was missing. Whoever had been there had just been a curious snooper, apparently. All the same, it worried us.

"It must have been somebody in Harmon Muldoon's gang," said Dinky Poore. "Nobody else would have feet that dirty."

"Very good thinking!" said Mortimer, with his usual sarcasm.

"I bet they're planning an act of sabotage," said Freddy, darkly.

"I don't think they'd be that foolish," said Henry. "Whoever came in here was a pretty good swimmer. We know that. And he also had to be pretty curious. If it was somebody from Harmon's gang, I'd say they were just green with envy and wanted to get a look inside the sub."

"Don't be too sure," warned Freddy. "I wouldn't trust that Harmon with my pet snake."

"Let's stop worrying about *who* it is, and figure out what we're gonna do about it," said Jeff Crocker.

"Maybe Zeke would lend us Kaiser Bill and let him sleep in here every night," Homer suggested.

"That's a good idea," Jeff agreed, "but he needs him

down at the junkyard."

"I move that Freddy and Dinky sleep here every night until we're finished with the work," said Mortimer.

"I move that Mortimer Dalrymple take the sub down to the bottom of the lake every night and stay there until morning," said Freddy Muldoon.

"Good thinking!" said Dinky Poore.

"I appreciate the humor, but let's use our heads," said Henry. "There's only one entrance to this place, and it's easy enough to bug it so we know whether anybody wanders in here."

"Now you're talking!" said Jeff. "What do you think we should do, Henry?"

"All we have to do is rig an electronic eye across the mouth of the cave and tie it into our carrier current intercom system. We can run a line from here down to one of the power lines on the highway, and I'll hook a monitor into my receiver at home. If I get an alarm during the night I'll push the panic button."

What Henry suggested doing was very simple, since we already had our own private intercom net operating through the city power lines. This can be done for free and it's legal, as long as you don't exceed the maximum power limit with your transmitter. We knocked off work on the sub and spent the rest of the day scurrying around to get the necessary equipment together to rig up the alarm system.

It was that very night that the panic buzzer sounded in my room just after I had gotten to sleep. It was Henry on the line, and he told us somebody had already tripped the alarm in the cavern. We hadn't bugged the place any too soon. Henry switched the microphones we'd hidden in the cavern into the net, and we could hear the voices of some of Harmon Muldoon's gang. Stony Martin, who's a loudmouth, was shouting out phony orders with a thick German accent as though he was Count Hugo von Luckner himself. It made me sick just to hear him.

"Let's go, Henry!" said Jeff Crocker. "Everybody out to the cavern!"

I jumped into my pants, threw a shirt on, and shinnied down the drainpipe outside my window. It was then I remembered that my dad had locked my bicycle in the garage. He told me I couldn't use it for two days, because I had forgotten to mow the lawn. I stood there in the darkness by the side of the house, not knowing what to do except swear at myself. I called the old man a bunch of bad names, too, and kicked the side of the house a couple of times. After I'd cooled off, I thought about shinnying back up the drainpipe and calling one of the other kids on the intercom, but I knew they'd all be gone. I even thought about sneaking into my dad's bedroom and swiping the key to the garage. But I figured I might wake somebody up, and then I would be in the soup. So I kicked the house a couple of more times and took off down the driveway heading for Dinky Poore's house.

Dinky lives closest to me and I might just be able to catch him. He also is the smallest guy in the club, and I wouldn't mind pumping his bike all the way out to the falls with him riding the handlebars. I darted into the alley behind his house and clambered up onto the fence. It was pitch dark in his backyard and I couldn't see if his bike was still there or not. I gave the tomcat call and waited a few seconds. There wasn't any answer, so I gave it again, a little louder and longer. This time there was an answer. I was peering into the darkest corner of the yard, when all of a sudden something came flying out of an upstairs window in his house and crashed against the board fence right below my hands. I didn't wait around to find out what it was. I just took off down the alley, heading for Mammoth Falls on foot.

It must have taken me half an hour to get to the riverbank below the falls. All the other kids were sitting around under the big oak tree where we usually hide our bikes in the bushes, holding a council of war.

"Where on earth have you been?" Henry asked me. "We've been waiting half the night."

"Maybe his mother wouldn't let him out!" Mortimer jibed at me.

"Shut up!" I shot back, giving Mortimer a knuckle job on his right bicep. Then I lied. "I had a flat tire on my bike. I ran all the way here."

"Let's get going!" urged Jeff. "Indian file down the bank, then one at a time under the falls. Nobody goes into the cave until we've all made it to the ledge. Then we'll rush 'em together."

We stripped down to our shorts and Jeff handed out stink bombs, three to a man. "If you get a shot at one of them, try to hit him in the middle of the back. It's hardest to wash off there."

We started down the steep path to the river bed with Mortimer leading the way. I took my usual position at the rear of the file, right behind Dinky and Freddy. There wasn't any moon out, and it was so dark we had to feel our way along the path, hugging close to the rocky bank. My heart was thumping and I could hear Dinky and Freddy breathing heavily. Suddenly there was a loud rumbling noise followed by an ear-splitting crash like a clap of thunder. The ground shook violently and the whole riverbank seemed to heave up about a foot. We grabbed for rocks and bushes and clung to the bank to keep from falling into the water. My head was swimming for a minute.

"Holy mackerel!" shouted Mortimer. "Half the falls has collapsed!"

"Let's get out of here before something else cuts loose," Jeff hollered. "Get back up the path, Charlie!"

I turned and groped my way back up the path to the top of the bank, with Freddy and Dinky panting behind me. When the rest of them got to the top, we made our way along the bank to a point where we could get a better look at the falls. By the light of our flashlights we could see a huge, crescent-shaped space at the lip of the falls that hadn't been there before. A regular torrent of water was spilling over it and crashing onto a pile of rocks at the bottom, right where the mouth of the cavern had been.

"The cavern's blocked off!" cried Mortimer. "If Harmon's gang is still in there, how are they gonna get out?"

"Serves 'em right for nosing around," said Freddy

Muldoon, jumping up and down.

"Oh, you're just full of the milk of human kindness," Mortimer sneered. "We gotta get down there and help 'em."

"Wait a minute!" Jeff cautioned. "Nobody's going down there just yet. We can't tell what might happen. Some more of that ledge might break loose any minute. We're just lucky we weren't all in there when it fell."

"We would have been if Charlie hadn't been late getting here," said Dinky Poore.

"Hurray for good old Charlie!" said Freddy Muldoon.

All of a sudden I wasn't mad at my old man, anymore, for locking my bike in the garage.

"We can't possibly move those rocks," Henry put in. "They're too big. The first thing we better do is call the police."

"How do we know they're still in there?" said Homer, "We'd look pretty foolish bringing the police out on a wild goose chase this time of night."

"That's easy enough to find out," said Henry. "We'll tap into the intercom line and see if we can talk to them."

"If they did anything to our submarine I hope they all drown," said Freddy Muldoon.

"What are we gonna do with these stink bombs?" asked Dinky Poore.

"Eat them!" said Mortimer. "You might not get any breakfast! Now, shut up and let the brains of this outfit figure out what we're gonna do."

Henry's foresight had provided a plug-in jack in the

intercom line at the top of the river bank. The only question was whether the line had been broken by the rock fall. Henry and Mortimer probed through the bushes and rocks at the edge of the falls and found the jack. Then they plugged in Henry's handset.

"Hello! Hello!" Henry called into the speaker. "This is Henry Mulligan. This is Henry Mulligan. If you can hear me, sing out!"

We all waited, holding our breath and straining to listen for a sound from the receiver. There was none.

"If they're still in there you probably scared them right out of their skins," said Homer. "Try it again."

Henry pressed his lips close to the handset. "This is Henry Mulligan calling Harmon Muldoon. Calling Harmon Muldoon. If you can hear me, get on the intercom. There's a speaker strapped under the diving board by the pool, and another one in the ceiling near the cave entrance. If you're still in there, let us know, so we can get help."

We waited for what seemed a full minute. Then we heard a crackling noise.

"Hello! Hello! Is that you, Harmon?" Henry repeated several times.

"Hello! This is Harmon Muldoon," came a voice so faint that only Henry could really hear it. "What do you want, Mulligan?"

"Thank God the line's still open!" Henry said excitedly. Then he cupped his hand around the mouthpiece. "He wants to know what we want."

"How do you like that fat-lipped cousin of mine!" snorted Freddy Muldoon. "There he is, buried a hundred feet underground, and he wants to know what we want."

"Tell him we want to know if they're all right, and how many of them are in there." said Jeff.

"Harmon! Harmon! Are you all right?" Henry shouted into the mouthpiece.

"Yeah, we're all right," came the faint answer. "What kind of a stunt did you guys pull on us this time?"

"Honest Injun, Harmon, we didn't do anything," Henry answered. "Part of the ledge at the top of the falls collapsed. There's a big pile of rocks blocking the mouth of the cave."

"Are you telling me?" sneered Harmon. "Have you got any other old news, Mulligan?"

"Oh, boy! Would I like to punch him right in the nose!" said Freddy.

"By the way, Mulligan," came Harmon's voice again, "how did you know we were in here?"

"There's an electronic eye at the mouth of the cave," Henry answered. You guys tripped it when you went in and it set off an alarm on our intercom."

"Very clever!" said Harmon. "I guess we never will outsmart you guys. Now, how do we get out?"

"How many of you are in there?" asked Henry.

"There are six of us," said Harmon. "Is that enough to qualify?"

"We'll get hold of the police right away," said Henry. "I don't know how they're going to get through to you, but we'll figure out some way. Sure you're all right?"

"Yeah! We're all right. It's fine in here. Just get us out in time for breakfast."

"He doesn't sound very scared for a guy trapped in a cave," said Homer.

"He's a cool character, all right," said Mortimer Dalrymple. "Something sounds a little fishy to me."

"It's Harmon's deep voice," said Freddy. "He's a big-mouthed bass."

Mortimer grabbed him by the collar and rubbed his knuckles in his hair good and hard.

Since we hadn't bothered leaving anybody at the clubhouse in Jeff Crocker's barn, we had no way of reaching the police except to ride into town and call them from the nearest phone we could get to. Jeff and Mortimer volunteered to make the trip, and the rest of us busied ourselves making as complete a reconnaissance as we could of the situation around the mouth of the cave. It would take Jeff and Mortimer at least fifteen minutes to get into town, and we knew it would be at least half an hour after that before Chief Putney could rouse any of his men and get them out to the falls. From the looks of things, they wouldn't be able to do anything without heavy equipment, so it would probably be hours before they mustered enough help to begin a rescue operation.

Literally tons and tons of rock had crashed down in front of the cave mouth, as far as we could tell from shining our flashlights onto the pile. The lip of the falls had receded to the point that one of the main plumes at the right of the torrent was spilling huge volumes of water directly down at the mouth of the cavern. It was possible that water was flowing into the cave.

Henry got on the intercom and roused Harmon

again. "Harmon!" he shouted. "Is water coming into the cave? Are you all right?"

"We're fine," Harmon answered. "It's dry as a bone in here. Now will you stop bothering us? We're trying to get some sleep. Just concentrate on getting us out of here."

"Okay!" said Henry. "But keep somebody near the intercom so we can keep in touch with you."

"Roger!" said Harmon.

"Those guys can *sleep*?" said Homer in disbelief.

"What else can they do?" Henry shrugged. "They have to wait for help, and they might as well save their strength. They might need it. You gotta hand it to them that they didn't panic."

Soon we heard the wailing of a siren and a screech of brakes as a police car pulled up nearby on the highway. Two officers came panting along the path, with Jeff and Mortimer leading them.

"How do you know there's anyone in there?" asked one of the officers, shining his flashlight into the abyss at the foot of the falls.

"We've talked to them," said Henry, and he explained about the intercom system. "You can talk to them if you want to," he offered.

"Never mind!" said the officer. "Looks like we've really got a job on our hands here." He whistled in surprise as he played his flashlight over the rockfall. "Holy mackerel! There must be tons of that stuff. It'll take real heavy construction equipment to move that stuff, and I don't know how anybody could get it down there to do the job. Are those kids safe in there?"

"They're all right, so far," said Henry.

The officer played his flashlight along the crest of the falls.

"Some more of that ledge could break loose any minute," he said. "If it does, the roof of that cave might collapse."

"That's possible," Henry agreed.

"We don't have any time to waste," said the officer, turning to the other policeman. "Al, get back to the car and tell Chief Putney he'd better notify the mayor. We've got a real emergency on our hands. Tell him we recommend putting out a general alarm and a request for rescue equipment. Better get the Civil Defense people out, too."

The other policeman turned to run up the path.

"Wait a minute, Al. After you call in, see if you can bust down a section of that fence and pull the car in here, somehow. We ought to have the radio right here."

"We'll bust down the fence!" cried Jeff. And he and Mortimer dashed up the path after the policeman.

It's amazing how fast things can happen sometimes. Within an hour the riverbank was swarming with people and vehicles. And more kept coming all the time, as calls went out for special equipment that somebody thought might help solve the problem of how to burrow through tons of rock with tons of water spilling on it, on the other side of a dangerous whirlpool more than a hundred feet offshore. There was a lot of confusion and shouting, and not much being accomplished, but it was exciting to watch.

The county sheriff's mobile rescue unit had pulled in

and flooded the area with high-powered searchlights. Seth Emory, the Civil Defense director, was supposed to be in charge of the operation, but Mayor Scragg did more talking than he did. He kept shouting orders to Chief Putney and to the fire chief, Hiram Pixley, telling them to do things that they were already doing; and he agreed with everybody's ideas about how to get into the cave, no matter how crazy they were. Somebody suggested bringing a long-boomed crane in with a clamshell bucket to lift some of the rocks away from the cave mouth. But a construction foreman who had been called out said the biggest crane they could get wouldn't reach out to the rockfall from the riverbank, and it would take at least two days to build a pier out into the water for the crane to operate from. Somebody else suggested running a pontoon bridge out to the rock pile and trying to force a hole through the rocks so a long section of corrugated iron storm drain could be run into the cave as an escape tunnel. But this was considered too dangerous, since more of the overhanging ledge might come plunging down at any minute. There were other people in favor of stringing a breeches buoy across the front of the falls so a couple of men could try to pull some of the rocks away with grappling hooks, but this was considered impractical. Some suggested taking a chance by trying to dynamite the rock pile, but almost everybody was against this.

A reporter and a photographer from the Mammoth Falls *Gazette* were circulating among the crowd, interviewing officials and getting opinions from onlookers. The reporter wanted to talk to the boys in the cave and Mayor Scragg said, "Sure! All you have to do is figure out how to get in there."

"But I thought there was some kind of a communication line into the cave," said the reporter. "One of the policemen told me—"

"I don't know about that," said the mayor. "You'll have to ask those young magicians over there. They're the ones that got us into this mess."

"I don't think they want to be bothered. They're all asleep," said Henry, when the reporter asked him. "Besides, I heard there's a camera crew coming from the TV station in White Fork. Why don't we wait until they get here?"

The reporter howled in anguish. "I was here first!" he complained. "I have to get my copy in for a special edition. If you make me miss it, and the TV stations get the story first, my boss will fire me!"

"Oh!" said Henry.

"Gosh, mister, we wouldn't want you to get fired over a little thing like six kids trapped in a cave," said Freddy Muldoon.

"I didn't mean it that way," said the reporter. "But this is a big story, and it's happening right in our backyard. Did you see what the TV networks did with that little girl that was trapped in a well out in Omaha last month? They kept the whole nation glued to their TV sets for three days. Can you imagine what they'll do when they have six kids trapped in a cave?"

"Yeah! I can imagine!" said Mortimer.

"Well? Do I get to talk to the kids?"

Henry shrugged.

"Say, what is this?" said the reporter truculently. "Are you in charge here?"

"No, I'm not in charge," said Henry, "but it's my intercom set."

"Oh! I get it!" The reporter reached for his wallet. "How would five bucks do?"

"You just said the magic word," said Freddy Muldoon.

"I don't want your money, mister," said Henry, pushing his hand in Freddy's face. "Wait until the TV crew gets here and we'll let everybody talk to them at the same time."

The reporter threw his hands in the air and turned

away. Then a thought struck him, and he pulled the photographer to one side. In a voice loud enough for everyone to hear he said, "What do you bet there aren't any kids down in that cave at all? You know, it's just possible these kids framed the whole thing."

"Hey, that's right!" said the photographer. "We don't know there's anybody down there. Say! That'd make a pretty good story too. Look at all these people here, and—"

Jeff stepped over to Henry. "I think maybe we'd better let 'em talk to Harmon."

"Okay!" said Henry. "I guess we'd better."

He managed to get Harmon to answer on the intercom after some trouble, and the reporter talked with him. Harmon said he was fine and gave him the names of the other five members of his gang that were with him. He woke up Stony Martin and had him talk to the reporter too. The photographer held the microphone of a tape recorder to the speaker while they were talking and taped the whole conversation.

"Are you worried about getting out?" asked the reporter.

"Naw! We're not worried," said Harmon.

"I'm sure they'll have you out in fine shape very soon," said the reporter, cheerfully.

"Tell 'em to take their time," said Harmon, yawning. "As long as we get home in time for breakfast, it's okay."

"Boy! Have we got a story!" crowed the reporter, as he stuffed his notes into his pocket. " 'Tell 'em to take their time,' the kid says. Can you imagine it? Boy! The wires'll eat this up!"

"Hey! I bet we could peddle this tape to all the networks!" said the photographer, as they hustled up the path to the highway.

"Aren't you going to stick around to see if they get out?" Mortimer shouted after them.

"Sorry!" the reporter shouted back. "We got a deadline to meet."

And they were gone.

"What a creep!" said Dinky Poore.

By the time the TV crew arrived from White Fork, things had reached an impasse. Some men had been sent out in small boats to reconnoiter the ledge below the falls to see if it were possible to anchor cables there so fire ladders could be run out from the shore. But they came back reporting no success. Mayor Scragg had called a conference under the big oak tree to get opinions on what would be the best way to proceed. It appeared that the most feasible plan would be to build some kind of footing in the creek bed for the big construction crane to work from. The mayor was asking for estimates on how long it would take to truck in enough rock and heavy fill to do this and whether it was possible to get the big crane down the steep bank with a block-and-tackle rig. Seth Emory had proposed that the city requisition every truck in the area and set up a high-speed shuttle with police escorts from the gravel pits out on White Fork Road. The estimates ran from half a day to a full day before real rescue operations could start.

Meanwhile, the director of the TV crew had been

pacing up and down at the edge of the group, running his fingers through his hair and looking at his watch every thirty seconds. He stepped over to Mayor Scragg and tapped him on the shoulder.

"Does that mean there won't be anything happening until noontime... or maybe even later?"

"If you mean when will we be getting the boys out, I guess that's it," said the mayor.

"We might as well pack up and go back and get some sleep, boys," said the director to the other members of his crew.

"Suit yourself," said Mayor Scragg. "I expect we'll be here a long time."

"As long as we're here, why don't we get some local color?" one of the cameramen suggested.

"Yeah! Maybe we could," said the director, rubbing his chin. "Say! That gives me an idea." He turned back to the mayor. "Is there any possible way to lower a camera into that cave?" he asked.

Mayor Scragg looked at him goggle-eyed. "If I could figure that out I could get those kids out," he said testily. "Now go away and stop bothering me!"

The director stepped back, a little abashed, and felt somebody plucking at his sleeve. It was Jeff Crocker.

"Excuse me, mister," he said. "There is a way to get a camera into the cave. But it would take a lot of cable, and it would have to be waterproof."

The director looked at Jeff, not knowing whether to believe him or not. "How much cable?" he asked.

Jeff shrugged. "Maybe three or four hundred feet. I don't know for sure."

"I hope you're not kidding me," said the director. "We don't have that much cable, but we could send and get it. Are you sure you could get it in there?"

"Yeah, I'm sure we could get it in there," said Jeff. "There is another way into the cavern, but you have to..." Then Jeff started rubbing *his* chin. "Wait a minute!" he said excitedly, and came running over to where the rest of us were. "Henry!" he said, grabbing him by the shoulder. "I'll bet we could get those kids out the same way we took the sub in, if we have enough diving gear!"

"Not so loud!" Mortimer cautioned, looking back to where the TV director was standing.

"Yeah!" said Freddy. "You'll give away our whole secret, blabbermouth!"

"Shut up, Freddy!" said Jeff, pushing him in the face. "The first thing we have to think about is getting Harmon and his gang out of there."

"We could go back and get our scuba gear," Mortimer suggested, "and Jeff and I could swim in there and bring 'em out one at a time."

"You could bring 'em out faster if you used the submarine," said Dinky.

"That's a good idea," Henry observed. "At least it's worth a try. We'd better talk it over with Mayor Scragg."

"You guys are gonna blow the whole thing!" screamed Freddy. "The whole town's gonna find out about our secret passage, and Harmon too!"

"What's all the argument about?" asked the TV director, walking over to where we stood. "Can you get a camera down there or not?"

"Forget your camera, mister," said Jeff, as we moved off to see the mayor under the oak tree. "We've got something more important to think about."

"What was that you said about a secret passage?" the director asked, grabbing Freddy by the arm.

"What secret passage?"

"A secret passage into that cave, you ninny!"

"Oh, *that* secret passage! That's none of your business," said Freddy, pulling his arm loose and running after us.

"Yes, Mulligan. What is it now?" said Mayor Scragg wearily, when Henry tapped him on the shoulder.

"We know of a way to get those kids out of there," Henry said simply, and he went on to explain how we had gotten the submarine into the cavern through a subterranean channel that ran under the cliff beside the falls and connected with the pool in the cavern.

"It's only about two hundred feet long," Jeff explained. "We discovered it one day when we were skin diving. The entrance is about ten feet underwater, and it's right where you want to dump all that rock to make a pier for the shovel. If you dump a lot of rock in there you'll probably block it up."

Mayor Scragg looked at them quizzically. "Every time I listen to you kids I get into more trouble!" he moaned, holding his hand to his forehead. "Isn't it enough that you've got half the town out here in the middle of the night?"

"Don't listen to a word they say, Mr. Mayor," said Freddy tersely, as he elbowed his way into the group. "It's all a big fat lie!"

"I told you to keep out of this!" said Jeff, pushing him in the face again. Freddy bounced right back and kicked Jeff in the shins. Mortimer grabbed him by the shoulders and pulled him off to the side.

"Cool it, Freddy!" he said, dumping him like a sack of potatoes. "Jeff knows what he's doing."

"He's a big blabbermouth!" Freddy blubbered. "He's giving away all our secrets."

"Secrets, huh?" said Mayor Scragg. "You mean you really do have a submarine down in that cave?"

"Honest Injun!" said Jeff. "You can ask Zeke Boniface. We brought it here in his truck."

"And you got it in there through an underground channel?"

"We didn't carry it in!" said Jeff.

The mayor thought this over for a while. Then he turned to talk with Seth Emory. Chief Putney and Chief Pixley joined them, and the four held a whispered consultation near the head of the path leading down to the water's edge. Finally the mayor beckoned to Henry and Jeff.

"We've got to do something and do it soon," he said. "You think you can swim in there and bring those boys out through that channel. Is that right?"

"Right!" said Jeff. "If they know how to use scuba gear, we'll get them to swim out. If they can't, we'll try using the submarine."

"It's worth a try," said the mayor, "but I'm going to send two men from the sheriff's rescue unit with you. We don't want any accidents."

"That's a good idea," said Jeff. "We can show them

the way. But we'll have to go back to town and get our tanks. We keep all that stuff in my barn."

"No need for that," said Chief Pixley. "The rescue unit has plenty of diving gear and everything else you'll need."

"Good deal," said Jeff. "That'll save time." And he and Mortimer started stripping down to their shorts. We didn't know it at the time, but if Jeff and Mortimer had gone to the clubhouse for their scuba outfits it would have saved us a lot of trouble.

Now that some definite action was being taken, the atmosphere along the creek bank changed abruptly.

You could feel the excitement generated in the rescue workers and onlookers as word spread among them that two kids had volunteered to swim into the blocked cavern through an underground waterway that nobody knew existed. Everybody crowded around the mobile rescue unit to watch the preparations.

The two sheriff's deputies fitted tanks and face masks on Jeff and Mortimer, and then the four of them linked themselves together with a piece of nylon line. It was decided that Jeff would lead the way and Mortimer would bring up the rear and feed out communication wire from a reel, so they would have direct communication with the mobile rescue unit, as well as a guideline for finding their way back out through the channel. The two deputies each carried an extra set of scuba gear, and all four were equipped with a flashlight and a knife.

The TV director was in a better humor, now, and kept getting in the way and delaying things as he tried to get as much of the action as he could on film. He started giving directions as to just how each man was to go down the path and get into the water, until Chief Putney pulled him gently aside and assigned two officers to keep him company for the duration of the operation.

Jeff waded into the water first. "Keep a tight line," he told the deputy behind him. "There are a lot of sharp rocks jutting out from the walls. We'll stay right on the bottom as much as possible. There's good white sand on the floor of the passage, and it's easier to see." Then he fitted his mask to his face, blew out a lungful of air, and opened the valve of his air tank. One by one the others followed him as he let himself out into deeper water and dove for the bottom. Soon there was nothing to be seen but a trail of air bubbles on the surface of the creek and the communication wire flapping up and down as it unreeled itself from the spool Mortimer was carrying.

For the watchers on the shore there was nothing to do but wait now, while the four divers probed the darkness of the underground channel. Everybody except the men in the mobile rescue van had crowded along the bank, pushing and shoving each other in an effort to get a better vantage point from which to watch the dark patch under the cliff where the trail of air bubbles had disappeared. Two people slipped and tumbled down the bank into the waters of the creek. Except for shining flashlights in their eyes, nobody paid much attention to them. The TV director was moaning about not being able to send a TV camera into the cavern with the divers. But Chief Pixley solved his problem by offering him a set of diving apparatus so he could take the camera in himself. The director decided that it wasn't that important.

Henry and the rest of us stayed glued to the side of the mobile rescue van, alongside Mayor Scragg. We knew that the first word from the four divers had to come in there through the communication line they had taken with them. It seemed like hours, but it was only ten minutes later that the deputy monitoring the phone line waved frantically for silence.

"Hello! Hello!" he said. "Is that you, Foster?" He listened for a moment. "Roger! We'll stand by. We're all ready up here."

"They've gotten through to the cave, and they're looking for the boys now," he told the mayor.

"Just ask them if there's a submarine in there," said Mayor Scragg, looking suspiciously at Henry.

The deputy whistled down the phone line again. "Hello, Foster! The mayor wants to know if there's a submarine in there?"

"Yeah, there's a submarine here all right," came the answer, "but there's no sign of any kids. We've looked all over the place. There's just nobody in here."

"Say that again?"

"I say there's no sign of any kids in here. I think there's something fishy about this whole thing."

"Did you hear that, Mr. Mayor?" said the deputy. "Foster says there's nobody in that cave!"

"Nobody in there?" exclaimed the mayor.

"Nobody in there?" echoed Henry.

The mayor turned and looked at Henry. "Mulligan..." he said.

"But there's got to be somebody in there!" Henry protested. "We talked to them on the intercom."

"Mulligan...!" said the mayor.

Henry turned and ran. He headed for the intercom jack at the base of the cliff, with the rest of us high-tailing it after him. The mayor and Chief Putney came puffing up the path behind us.

"Jeff! Jeff!" Henry hollered into the handset. "Can you hear me in there?"

"We hear you loud and clear!" came Jeff's voice in reply.

"What about Harmon and his gang? Where are they?"

"I don't know where they are, but they're sure not in here! We've searched the whole place."

"Scout's honor, Jeff?"

"Scout's honor, Henry!"

"I just don't understand it," said Henry, helplessly. "We were talking to them not more'n half an hour ago."

Henry was still standing there, scratching his head and looking crestfallen when the mayor and Chief Putney broke through the bushes.

"Well Mulligan, what's this all about?" puffed the mayor, all out of breath.

"They're just not in there, Mr. Mayor," said Henry, dejectedly. "I don't understand it. They were there just half an hour ago."

"Why don't you tell 'em the truth, Mulligan?" came Harmon Muldoon's voice from somewhere in the darkness above us. "You know we weren't in that cave." A chorus of raucous laughter almost drowned out the last words. Henry's jaw dropped open as he stared upward through the darkness toward the lip of the cliff that towered above us.

"Who's that up there?" Chief Putney demanded, as he flashed his powerful light along the edge of the cliff.

"Pretty good show, Mulligan!" came the strident voice of Stony Martin. "Whatta ya do for an encore?" And another wave of raucous laughter followed.

It was obvious that Harmon's whole gang was sitting up on the cliff above our heads watching the proceedings with great relish. The glare from the floodlights on the rescue van was too bright for us to see into the darkness, but finally Chief Putney's flashlight picked out the white T-shirt of Stony Martin, perched in a tree. Stony scrambled back into the shadow with a burst of mocking laughter. A lot of raspberries and other uncouth sounds split the darkness.

"How did you get up there?" Henry shrilled, rather weakly.

"We walked up!" Harmon shouted back.

"I mean, how did you get out of the cavern?"

"That was simple! We weren't in the cavern."

"Aw, c'mon, Harmon. Somebody was in there."

"Yeah, we sent one man in to trip your alarm so we could raid your clubhouse. We've been up in Crocker's barn all night."

"You mean you were in our clubhouse all the time when we were talking on the intercom?"

"Yeah, after we tripped your alarm system all kinds of things began to happen. It was rich!"

Henry just stood there, speechless. He didn't even hear Mayor Scragg and Chief Putney arguing about whether they should arrest anybody, as they beat their way back through the bushes to the rescue van.

"By the way, Henry," Stony Martin shouted. "How do you get that cash box of yours down off that rafter? We spent most of the night trying to figure it out."

Henry didn't answer. He just threw the intercom set he was holding against the side of the cliff, and then kicked it into the bushes. It broke into a dozen pieces. I had never seen Henry lose his temper before.

Big Chief Rainmaker

It was one of those hot August days in Mammoth Falls when even the dogs won't go out on the street, and you don't dare open your mouth for fear of getting your tongue sunburned. I was sitting in old Ned Carver's barbershop, thumbing through a magazine and waiting for Mr. Carver to finish cutting Charlie Brown's hair, when Jason Barnaby stumbled in through the door and flopped down in a chair to fan himself.

"How's the apples look this year, Jason?" mumbled Charlie Brown through the hot, wet towel wrapped around his face. Jason's apple orchard up on Brake Hill is the biggest orchard in the county. It's a regular showpiece for visitors.

"Ain't gonna be no apples if we don't soon get some rain," whined Jason, moping his gray hair back off his forehead. "I never did see such a hot spell as we're havin' now."

"Yes, sir!" Ned Carver agreed. "That little piece of grass in front of my place is about burned to a crisp right now. I expect it's been a month since we've seen a real rain."

"Longer'n that," moaned Jason. "Them leaves on my trees'll snap right in two in your fingers, they're so dry."

"I hear tell Mayor Scragg is bringin' in some professional rainmakers," said Charlie Brown. "Some real experts from the Department of Agriculture and the State University."

"Won't do no good," muttered Jason, stoically. "They tried that over in Clinton last year, and it wasn't worth a hill of beans—all them birds with their blowin' machines and their silly airplanes! Pshaw! You might as well get down on your knees and pray. When the Lord says 'Let it rain!' it'll rain."

"That don't say you can't give the Lord a helpin' hand," said Charlie. "The mayor and the town council know what they're doing." Charlie Brown is the town treasurer and he's been on the town council for thirty-one years. He also owns the only funeral parlor in Mammoth Falls, and everybody respects him. He generally knows what's going on in town.

Jason Barnaby didn't answer for a while. He was staring at the highly polished toes of Charlie's black pumps.

"How come you're always wearing a new pair of shoes?" he asked, finally. "I swear you got more shoes than any man in town."

"Mind your own business!" said Charlie Brown. "We were talkin' about the dry spell."

I didn't hear much of the rest of the conversation, because I kept falling asleep like I always do in the barbershop—especially on hot days. I woke up when Mr. Carver snapped the hair cloth and said "Next!"

"Couldn't you Mad Scientists do something to bring

on rain?" he asked me with a chuckle, as I climbed into the chair. "You kids are always getting mixed up in something crazy."

"I s'pose if anybody could make it rain, Henry Mulligan could," I said, before I fell asleep again. Old Ned Carver didn't know it, but he had started something. Before the month was out he was wishing he'd kept his mouth shut.

The Mad Scientists' Club meets almost every day during the summer, because we usually have some kind of a project going. When I went out to Jeff Crocker's barn that afternoon to find the rest of the gang, my head was full of crazy notions about how we might make it rain—like dipping a huge sponge in Strawberry Lake and floating it over Mr. Barnaby's apple orchard suspended from big balloons.

In the clubhouse I found Mortimer Dalrymple fiddling around with the ham radio outfit and Homer Snodgrass stretched out on the rusty old box spring mattress in the corner reading a tattered volume of Rudyard Kipling's poetry.

"Hey, listen to this!" said Homer.

> " 'If you can keep your head when all about you
> Are losing theirs and blaming it on you,
> If you can trust yourself—' "

"If I had your head I wouldn't want to keep it!" said Mortimer in a loud voice.

Homer answered him with a raspberry and rolled over to prop his book against the wall.

"Where's Henry and Jeff?" I asked. "I got important business to discuss."

"They're out in back, washing Mr. Crocker's car," said Mortimer.

Jeff Crocker's dad makes him wash the family car once a week. We're all supposed to help in return for using the barn as our clubhouse, but mostly Jeff ends up washing it himself. Fortunately, he and Henry were just about finished when I found them, and I told them all about the conversation I had heard in the barbershop.

"I know it's been rough," Jeff said. "All the farmers around here are complaining. My dad says there won't be enough hay to feed the horses this winter if it doesn't rain soon."

"It's easy enough to make it rain," said Henry. "All you have to do is create the proper conditions." Henry stopped wiping off the car, and I could see he was thinking about the problem. I finished the last fender for him.

"When are these professional rainmakers coming?" he asked me.

"I don't know. But Homer's father should know, 'cause he's on the town council."

"I suggest we don't do anything until after they've been here," said Jeff, as he spread the rags out to dry. "After all, the town is probably paying them a lot of money, and they might just make it rain."

"What do you think, Henry?" I asked.

"I think I've got an idea!" said Henry, and he walked straight down the lane to the main road and went home, and we didn't see him again for three days—which isn't unusual when Henry is thinking.

The rainmakers came, and we all went out to watch them set up their machines. They had huge blowers that they used to create a white fog of dust particles in the air, and they set them up on the hills all around the valley. They also had two light airplanes operating out of the county airport that they'd send up to seed the rain clouds whenever any appeared.

Dinky Poore was as inquisitive as usual.

"What's that white stuff they're blowin' into the air?" he asked Henry.

"That's silver iodide crystals," said Henry. "They're supposed to make water vapor condense and form into drops of water. The trouble is, you've got to have water vapor to start with, and the air's so dry right now I don't think it'll do any good."

The rainmakers kept at it for two weeks, but they didn't do much good. They got a spat of rain now and then, but not enough to sneeze at. And every day they had a different excuse: the wind wasn't right, or there weren't enough clouds, or they couldn't get the airplanes into the air in time when a good cloud did appear. All in all, it was a pretty expensive operation, and the farmers were pretty skeptical about it and were grumbling about the cost. Finally, Mayor Scragg and the town council held a big public meeting where everybody had their say, and the general opinion seemed to be that rainmaking was for the birds. And when Charlie Brown declared that the town just couldn't afford any more rainmaking experiments, the whole idea was scrapped.

That was when Henry Mulligan decided it was time for the Mad Scientists' Club to act. We had a meeting in the clubhouse, and Henry outlined the plan to us.

"The trouble with most rainmakers," he said, "is that they spread themselves too thin. You can't go firing silver iodide crystals into the air willy-nilly. You've got to hit a particular cloud at a particular time, and you've got to concentrate a lot of stuff in one place, to do any good."

Henry pulled a long sleek-looking piece of tubing with fins on it from under the table and showed it to us.

"This is a pretty simple rocket," he said, "but it'll go up high enough to hit most rain clouds. Right here behind the nose cone is a cartridge with a little gunpowder in it and a lot of silver iodide crystals. All you have to do is explode the cartridge at the right time and spray the crystals through the cloud. Grape growers in northern Italy have been using these for twenty years to make it rain on their vineyards. They just wait until a likely-looking cloud comes along, and then they blast away at it."

"Holy mackerel!" said Freddy Muldoon. "You think of everything, Henry."

"I didn't think of it," said Henry. "I just read a lot."

"So do I," said Homer Snodgrass, "but I never seem to read the right stuff."

"You don't learn much from that poetry; that's a cinch!" said Mortimer.

"You do, too! You just don't understand it!" declared

Homer stoutly.

"How high up will that rocket go?" asked Dinky Poore.

"That depends on how we design it," said Henry. "Most rain-bearing clouds form at about five thousand feet. It's simple enough to calculate the size of the rocket and the amount of fuel we need to lift a cartridge of silver iodide to that altitude. If we figure the motor burning time correctly we don't have to use any timing mechanism to explode the cartridge. The heat of the propellant will do it."

"Let's try it!" said Dinky Poore, eagerly. Dinky's always ready to try anything.

"First we've got to build the rockets," said Henry. "This is just a preliminary design. We've got to flight test a few before we know whether we have the right design."

The next few days we were busy as beavers. We'd spend half the night building rockets in our machine shop, up in the loft over Mr. Snodgrass's hardware store, and then we'd pedal out to a spot in the hills west of Strawberry Lake to test-fire them during the day. We fired them in a steep trajectory, slightly off the vertical, so the spent rocket bodies would land in the lake. By watching for a splash as the rocket hit the surface of the water, we could get a pretty precise measurement from launch to impact. From this, Henry could tell us exactly how high the rocket was going.

After we had fired about twenty rockets of different types, Henry declared himself satisfied that we had the right design. Then we set to work and built about thirty rockets, complete with cartridges filled with silver iodide crystals. We designed them so the fins would fit snugly inside a piece of corrugated rain spout which would serve as the launching tube. We used a mixture of powdered zinc and sulphur as the propellant and fitted each rocket with an electrical squib for an igniter. We could have launched them by lighting a fuse with a match, but Henry said this wasn't safe. In case one blew up, he wanted everyone to be a safe distance away. So we rigged up a firing circuit with dry cell batteries to ignite the squib.

"Now whatta we do?" asked Freddy Muldoon, when we had finished the last rocket.

Everybody looked at Jeff, who gives most of the orders because he's president, and Jeff looked at Henry.

"I think we've got to prove we can do what we think we can do, first," said Henry. "Let's set up on Brake Hill near Mr. Barnaby's orchard and stake a lookout there all day long. If any clouds come over, and we can hit one and make it rain, then maybe we can expand our operations."

"I'm for that!" said Freddy, rubbing his pudgy stomach. "I'll volunteer for lookout."

"Good!" said Jeff. "The lookout will have to go all the way to the top of the hill to watch for clouds. That'll keep you away from the apples."

"Let the minutes reflect that I withdraw my offer," said Freddy.

"Noted, but not approved!" said Homer, who was taking notes. "It doesn't make any difference, anyway.

Most of Jason Barnaby's apples are Baldwins, and they're still too green to eat."

"You're talking to the champion green apple eater of Mammoth County!" said Freddy Muldoon.

The next morning we all packed a lunch and set out bright and early for Brake Hill with a supply of rockets and a couple of launching tubes. Mortimer and Freddy went to the top of the hill with a radio to set up the cloud watch. But Freddy kept sneaking down to snitch apples off the trees on the upper slopes of the orchard. By noontime he had such a stomachache that he was rolling on the ground, and Mortimer had to send him back down the hill to where we were. We just let him lie around and groan all he wanted to.

By early afternoon a lot of clouds had begun to form on the horizon and Mortimer reported a couple of big ones being blown in from the east, right toward Brake Hill. We got the launching tubes set up, pointing to where we thought the clouds would come over the brow of the hill, and waited.

In about an hour a big, puffy, white one loomed over us, and Henry checked out the firing circuit and then connected the batteries to the squib leads in the rocket nozzles. We waited until the bulk of the cloud had drifted directly over our heads. Then Henry said, "Fire number one!"

Jeff threw the switch to close the firing circuit and the first rocket swished into the sky, leaving a billowing cloud of smoke behind. We saw a bright flash, and a few seconds later we heard a sharp report like a large firecracker.

"That one exploded a little early; about forty-five-hundred feet," said Henry. "I counted just four seconds from the flash to the bang. The propellant must have burned too fast."

We saw the bright, silver flash of the rocket tube as it plunged down out of the cloud and caught the rays of the sun. We waited a long minute, but nothing happened. The huge cloud continued drifting slowly over us.

"Fire number two!" said Henry.

I threw my switch and the second rocket shot out of its launch tube with a hissing roar. It veered to the right momentarily, then straightened itself and plunged like a dart into the soft underbelly of the cloud. Suddenly the whole cloud turned a brilliant golden yellow as flaming particles shot through it in every direction. It looked as though a bolt of lightning had struck it. Henry was jumping up and down even before the report of the explosion had reached us, and Homer Snodgrass was slapping him on the back.

"A hit! A hit! A palpable hit!" cried Homer.

"Let's wait and see! Let's wait and see!" cried Henry, trying to ward of the blows.

It was then that we heard the *putt-putt-putt* of Jason Barnaby's rusty old Model T Ford and turned to see it weaving and bouncing toward us down the lane that led through the apple orchard. Jason's two German shepherd dogs were galloping along beside the old rattletrap, barking their heads off, and we could see a double-barreled shotgun clamped to the windshield. Jason brought the old puddle-jumper to a sputtering

halt in a cloud of dust and jumped down from the seat with the shotgun clenched in one fist.

"What in tarnation are you young rapscallions doin' here?" he shouted at us. "Are you stealin' my apples? What's them fireworks I been hearin'?"

Freddy, who had been lying on the ground, still writhing in pain, started crawling for the bushes at the edge of the orchard. Dinky Poore's eyes had popped wide open, and he was trembling like a leaf. Jeff Crocker stepped forward.

"We weren't doing anything, Mr. Barnaby," he

explained. "We were just trying to make it rain."

"Trying to make it rain? If that don't beat all!" exclaimed old Jason, whipping his hat off and slamming it onto the ground.

His face was redder than any apple in the orchard, and the veins in his neck stood out as though he were going to have a fit of apoplexy. When he bent over to pick up his hat, the startling contrast of the smooth, white top of his bald head made Mortimer Dalrymple burst out laughing.

"What are you laughing at, you young hyena?" Jason shouted. "If you think you can—"

Suddenly Jason clapped his hand to his bare head. "What's that?" he said. And he looked upward in time to catch another raindrop right in the corner of his left eye. He wiped it off with a fingertip. Then he stuck his tongue out and turned his face upward again. The drops started coming down more rapidly—big, splashy drops that splattered on the leaves of the apple trees and sent a cascade of tiny droplets in every direction. Jason spread his arms out with the palms of his hands turned upward and threw his head back. He held his battered old felt hat out in front of him, as if to catch the precious drops and hold them forever. He opened his mouth and tried to drink in the rain. Several large drops hit him right in the face, and a trickle of water zigzagged down the side of his weather-beaten neck and cut a channel through the dust that covered his skin. Suddenly he started to gyrate and cavort among the apple trees in a wild and spontaneous dance.

"Whoopee!" shouted old Jason. "It's rain, rain, rain! The rain's a fallin'. The rain's a fallin'."

And it was. It came down in a regular torrent. We looked upward and saw that the belly of the huge white cloud had broken open and dark streamers of water vapor were cascading toward the earth. We had started a regular cloudburst!

We scrambled to get all our gear together and pull it under the trees. The two German shepherds were prancing around after Jason and paying no attention to us.

"One thing we forgot to bring was umbrellas," said Mortimer.

"Not even Henry can think of everything," said Dinky Poore.

"You don't need no umbrellas!" came a voice from under the trees. "Get under that tarpaulin in the back of the Model T, and I'll ride you home."

We were soaked to the skin, but we laughed and shouted as we bounced back through the orchard in Jason's ancient pickup.

"Tarnation! If that don't beat all!" muttered Jason, as he wrestled with the wheel. "I think I'll crack open a jug of hard cider when I get back to the house."

It didn't take long for the word to get around town that we had made it rain on Jason's apple orchard. Old Jason drove us right into town and stopped off at Ned Carver's barbershop on his way home. In a small town the barbershop is better than the telephone exchange when it comes to rapid communication. Mayor Scragg was among the first to hear about it, and he stopped off at Henry's house that night and patted him on the head and called him "Big Chief Rainmaker."

Charlie Brown, the treasurer, was a little dubious, though. If we could make it rain every time a cloud came over, he wanted to know how much it was going to cost the town to keep us in business. Jeff assured him that we weren't interested in draining the town treasury. All we wanted to do was help the farmers save their crops, and if the farmers were willing to pay for the rockets and the zinc and sulphur we needed, the Mad Scientists' Club was at their service.

After that we were flooded with requests from farmers to set up rocket launchers on their property and try to make it rain. We couldn't take care of everybody, and we didn't want to play favorites, so we held a meeting in the clubhouse to figure out what to do. Dinky Poore made his usual suggestion about writing to the President for help and was voted down, as usual. Freddy Muldoon thought we could take care of everybody if we just ran fast enough from one farm to another.

"Great idea, Pudgy!" said Mortimer. "Only I don't see any Olympic medals hanging on *you*. By the time you get through breakfast, it's time for lunch. You sweat faster than you can run, and we wouldn't want you to drown."

"Okay, wise guy!" Freddy shot back. "At least when I step on a scale, something happens. I thought maybe I could stick around here and man the radio."

After a lot of discussion we made a revolutionary decision. For the first time in the history of the Mad Scientists' Club we decided to ask Harmon Muldoon's gang to help us out.

"This is a community project," Henry pointed out, "and there's no reason to be selfish about it."

"Nuts!" said Freddy. "My cousin will hog all the credit. Besides, he doesn't know anything about rockets."

"We can teach them all they have to know," said Jeff. "As far as the credit goes, everybody already knows who Big Chief Rainmaker is."

Then we all stood up and gave Henry the Indian sign, and that was the end of the meeting. Jeff Crocker was appointed ambassador plenipotentiary to conduct negotiations with Harmon Muldoon, because he can beat anybody in Harmon's gang at Indian wrestling. He didn't have to put the arm on them, though. They jumped at the opportunity to get into the act.

We set up several launching sites at strategic locations that gave us a chance to cover most of the farms in the valley on fairly short notice. With Harmon's equipment added to ours, we had a pretty good radio net operating from our clubhouse in Jeff Crocker's barn. We couldn't be everywhere at once, even with six two-man teams manning the launch sites; but we didn't have to worry about cloud watchers. Every farmer in the valley was bombarding us with phone calls each time a wisp of cloud appeared on the horizon.

We didn't keep count, but we must have fired about two hundred rockets during the next two weeks. We didn't make it rain every time, of course. Sometimes we might fire ten rockets before we got a good hit on a cloud. And sometimes, even when we got a good hit, nothing would happen. But we did manage to hit the jackpot often enough to make the difference between a dry year and a drought. Most everybody in town seemed to agree that Henry's idea had saved the farmers from a real crop failure. People he didn't even know would wave at Henry on the street and say, "How, Big Chief!"

The rest of us basked in Henry's reflected glory, of course, and we seemed to get more smiles from the storekeepers than usual. Even Billy Dahr, the town constable, looked as though he was glad to see us when one of us passed him on the street. And Jeff Crocker's dad was no exception. He was seen one day washing his own car, and he told a curious neighbor that he thought Jeff needed a rest.

But somehow I felt uncomfortable about it all, despite our success. I finally realized that it was because I once heard Henry say that you can't tamper with nature without getting into trouble. And it didn't take too long for Henry's observation to prove true.

Freddy Muldoon and Dinky Poore were manning the launch site out on Blueberry Hill one day when a cloud about ten times the size of the *Queen Elizabeth* came drifting over. They got all excited and started firing rockets at it as fast as they could mount them on the launcher. They weren't supposed to be out there, and there wasn't any sense in firing at the cloud so soon because it hadn't even gotten out over the valley yet. But they wanted to show what they could do, so they blasted away at it and finally scored a good hit. The cloud practically evaporated and dumped torrents of rain on the hilltop. Dinky and Freddy fell all over themselves in a mad scramble to get their ponchos on and pedal back into town to brag about what they had done.

When they got down to the road that leads past Memorial Point, where the old Civil War cannon is, they saw people streaming out of the woods by the hundreds, slipping and sliding down the hill with their arms full of blankets, tablecloths, picnic baskets, baseball bats, musical instruments, and beer kegs. The sudden cloudburst had broken up the annual Kiwanis Picnic and Songfest for the Benefit of Homeless Children and turned it into a rain-soaked rout.

Joe Dougherty, who is president of the Kiwanis Club and trombone soloist in the town band, was hopping mad. He complained loudly to Mayor Scragg that the whole thing was a deliberate plot by those troublemakers in the Mad Scientists' Club to ruin the annual picnic and sabotage the Kiwanis Club's fundraising program. He claimed that we had made it rain intentionally, in order to get back at the Kiwanis for refusing to sponsor our project to explore the bottom of Strawberry Lake. Henry and Jeff were called on the carpet by the mayor, and of course they denied having any such intentions. But that didn't change the fact that the Kiwanis picnic had been flooded out, and a strawberry shortcake the size of a bathtub had to be abandoned in the middle of the clearing at Memorial Point.

Far from bragging about their prowess as rainmakers, Freddy and Dinky were trying to deny any connection with the episode when Henry and Jeff got back to the clubhouse.

"We were down by Lemon Creek all the time," said Freddy, stoutly. "We didn't even know any Kiwanis picnic was going on... Honest Injun to that last part," he added, holding his right hand up.

Jeff Crocker fastened a gimlet eye on him. "Joe Dougherty claims they heard about five rockets fired just before it started to rain, and he has four hundred witnesses to back him up. Who do you think fired those rockets, Freddy?"

"Probably my cousin Harmon," said Freddy offhandedly, pretending that he saw something very interesting outside the window. "He's always sneaking around where he's not supposed to be."

"It so happens that Harmon was here in the clubhouse with us all the time," said Henry, quietly. "And the rest of his gang were assigned to man the launch sites south of town. I don't think it's very fair to try and blame this on Harmon."

"Okay! Okay!" said Freddy, thrusting the palms of his hands upwards. "So it didn't work!"

Our reputation managed to survive the episode of the Kiwanis picnic, but not for long. Mortimer Dalrymple and Homer Snodgrass sat out the Brake Hill watch one day at the edge of Jason Barnaby's apple orchard. It had been three days since any good clouds had been sighted in the valley, but there was a cool wind blowing in from the east that held promise of moisture to come.

It was about noontime that a big, black cloud came riding high over the crest of Brake Hill. It looked like a prime thunderhead, and Homer and Mortimer got the artillery ready. They hit it with two shots and ran for cover among the trees in the orchard. They hadn't yet reached the shelter of a tent they had strung between two of the trees when a deafening roar surrounded them.

"What was that?" cried Homer. "Something hit me!"

No sooner had he said it than a hailstone the size of a pullet egg hit him on the right shoulder.

"Geronimo!" cried Mortimer. "It's hailing doorknobs. Run for cover!"

They both dove under the tent while hailstones pelted the orchard all around them and apples came thumping to the ground by the hundreds. The accumulated weight of ice and Baldwin apples on the sagging eaves of the tent finally collapsed it, and the two of them lay flat on the ground holding the canvas above their heads for protection. The cloud was a big one and it drifted on through town, leaving a trail of minor destruction in its path, and finally spent itself in the hills across the valley.

A cast-iron straight jacket wouldn't have held Jason Barnaby still after that one. He barged into Mayor Scragg's office and thumped loudly on the mayor's desk, complaining that half his apple harvest had been ruined. He forgot all about the fact that he wouldn't have had any apples at all if we hadn't brought rain to his orchard in the first place. Abner Larrabee's wife, who is a social leader in town, wailed piteously in a letter to the editor of the Mammoth Falls *Gazette* that her prize peonies had been stoned to death just before they

reached the full glory of their bloom. She complained bitterly about "wanton boys who create mischief with their teen-age pranks" and wondered when the mayor was going to do something about the problem of juvenile delinquency.

The episode of the hailstorm seemed to dampen some of the enthusiasm for our project around town, but the more rain-thirsty farmers kept urging us to continue. The editor of the *Gazette* wrote an editorial in our defense, in which he pointed out that our intention had been to do the community a worthwhile service. And Henry admitted in an interview for the paper that we didn't know all the answers yet about how to cope with nature, but that any scientist knew that he faced certain risks whenever something new was being tried. He promised that we would try to learn all about hail clouds and avoid mistakes in the future.

A few days after the hailstorm, the town of Mammoth Falls awoke to find itself shielded from the sun by a low and heavy overcast. The temperature had dropped, and the hot spell seemed to be over. Everybody could smell rain in the wind, and the town looked forward to the end of the long summer drought. But still no rain came. For three days the overcast continued, and the atmosphere was heavy. The cattle were restless, and chicken farmers complained that the hens cackled all night and laid no eggs.

On the fourth day we held a meeting with all the members of Harmon Muldoon's gang, and everybody was in favor of giving nature the needle. We decided to launch six rockets simultaneously from different launch sites scattered around the valley to see if we could make the overcast give out with some rain. We set up the radio net, and Henry gave a countdown from the control center in our clubhouse. Five of the rockets fired perfectly and exploded within seconds of each other in the dense cloud cover. We later found out that Dinky Poore and Freddy Muldoon at the sixth site had an argument over who was going to push the firing button; after they both decided to let the other one push it, neither one would agree to do it. So the argument ended up in a stalemate.

"What's the matter?" asked Henry, when he was

finally able to get them on the radio.

"Nothin'!" said Dinky. "That stupid Freddy is just too dumb to push the button!"

It started to rain, all right. Nothing spectacular. Just a nice, steady downpour that drummed on the roofs of the town and soaked into the fields and meadows. The salvo of rockets had been heard all over town, of course, and Henry was kept busy in the clubhouse taking calls from farmers who wanted to let him know it was raining.

It rained all through that day and long into the night. Spirits were high in Mammoth Falls, and we were once more in the good graces of everyone. It was the first continuous rain of the summer, and the *Gazette* that afternoon offered a one-hundred-dollar prize to anyone who could correctly predict the number of inches that would fall. The next morning it was still raining with no sign of a letup. It looked odd to see umbrellas on the streets and people wearing rubbers. But nobody was grumbling about it, as they usually do when it's wet and nasty out. The downtown merchants were doing a good business despite the weather, and everyone was wearing a smile.

The smiles turned a little sour, though, by the time it had rained for four days straight. It's a funny thing, but no matter how badly people want rain, it doesn't take much of it to satisfy them—and not much more to make them gripe about the weather. By the end of the week everyone was asking when the rain would let up, and a lot of people were complaining about their cellars flooding. In Ned Carver's barbershop the talk was about nothing else but the rain, and about the mud-slides that were occurring in the hills. The *Gazette* was offering a two-hundred-dollar prize to anyone who could predict the exact hour the rain would stop.

It just kept raining. It didn't seem that the sun would ever come out again. By the tenth day there was serious concern in Mammoth Falls, and the town council was holding a special meeting to decide what to do about Lemon Creek. It was up over its banks already in some places, and a couple of the back roads that crossed it had been closed. Nobody could remember a flood in Mammoth Falls, but if the rain kept up, it looked as though we would have one.

Henry and Jeff and I were sitting in the drugstore across from the Town Hall having a malted milk when Mayor Scragg and some members of the council came in to get a sandwich. The mayor cleared his throat with a loud *harrumph*, as he always does when he's about to say something, and came over to where we were sitting.

"This is a fine mess you've gotten us into, Mulligan!" he said tersely.

"I'm sorry, Mr. Mayor, but I don't think it's our fault," said Henry, staring into his malted milk.

"Well, you made it rain, with your crazy scientific gimmicks! Isn't there some way you can stop it?" pleaded the mayor.

Henry shook his head dubiously, then looked at the mayor sideways. "We haven't gotten that far, yet!" he said, staring into his malted again.

The rest of the council members burst into laughter.

"Well, supposing you read up on it," said the mayor,

gruffly. "It looks as though we're going to have a serious flood."

"Nobody has ever figured out a way to make it *stop* raining," said Henry with an air of serious concentration. "That's one of the troubles with scientists. They know some of the answers, but not all of them. It just goes to show that you can tamper with nature, but you can't control her. She always strikes back."

"There must be something we can do!" said the mayor, turning away.

"Yes, there is!"

"What's that?"

"You can pray!"

"Not a bad idea!" said the mayor. "Supposing you start in!" And he went back to his table to munch his sandwich.

Somebody took Henry seriously, because the following Sunday there was a general day of prayer in all the churches in town. But it didn't do any good. Monday morning dawned with a leaden sky and brought the fifteenth consecutive day of rain on Mammoth Falls. The Civil Defense Corps had put out a call for volunteers to sandbag the banks of Lemon Creek so it wouldn't flood the business section. Some of the outlying streets north of town were already under water. We got all the members of Harmon Muldoon's gang together, and between us we had enough workers to take over one whole section of the dike building. Everybody in town who had a truck of any description was pressed into service, and by late afternoon Mayor Scragg had declared a state of emergency.

The work at the creek bank went on all through the night under the glare of searchlights which the Air Force had brought in from Westport Field. By midnight, Lemon Creek was a raging torrent of muddy, turbulent water. Even if we managed to contain the water within the sandbag dikes, there was danger that the swollen stream would wash away the principal bridge at the end of Main Street. Seth Emory, who is Director of Civil Defense, and Police Chief Harold Putney made a survey of the entire line of dikes and predicted that if it rained again on Tuesday the water would rise more rapidly than we could fill sandbags. A flood was almost certain, unless the rain let up.

In desperation, Mayor Scragg got on the telephone at his command post near the bridge. He called the State University and the United States Weather Bureau and got their expert meteorologists out of bed. When he asked them if they knew of any way to make it stop raining, they both said he must be some kind of a nut and slammed the phone down in his ear. The mayor, muddy and rain-soaked, turned away from the phone to confront Mrs. Abner Larrabee and the members of her garden circle, who had him hemmed in.

"Mr. Mayor," said Mrs. Larrabee, in the tone of voice women use when they think things have gone far enough, "what do you intend to do about the rain?"

Mayor Scragg buried his face in his hands and sobbed loudly, twice. Then he looked up, and a fiendish gleam leaped into his eyes. With magnificent self-control he said, "Mrs. Larrabee, I intend to give you authority to stop it!"

"Excellent!" said Mrs. Larrabee. "Then I have an announcement to make."

"Yes, Mrs. Larrabee," sighed the mayor. "What is your announcement?"

"The ladies of the Greater Mammoth Falls Garden Circle, of which I am president, and the ladies of the Mammoth Falls chapter of the Friends of the Wildwood, of which I am also president as well as corresponding secretary, have invited the members of the Daughters of Pocahontas and their husbands to join them in an ancient Indian sun dance. It is a ritual dance of the Pawnees, and one in which they had great faith."

"Yes, Mrs. Larrabee!"

"We intend to perform the dance at six A.M. tomorrow morning at Lookout Rock on the top of Indian Hill. It's a most appropriate place, don't you think?"

"Yes, Mrs. Larrabee!"

"We would like you and all the town council members to be there. We think the whole community should support us."

"I'm sure they will, Mrs. Larrabee."

"But will you be there, Mr. Mayor?"

"Yes!" said the mayor, wearily. "I might as well be. My house will probably be under water."

"And the members of the council?"

"Yes, Mrs. Larrabee. They will be there."

This was something we couldn't afford to miss. Tired as we were, we dragged ourselves to the top of Indian Hill in the half-gray light of the morning. We had worked all night on the dikes, and there was nothing more that could be done. If the creek rose any higher, the sheer weight of the water would burst the sandbag walls.

It was a motley crowd that assembled in the grassy clearing behind Lookout Rock that morning. A persistent drizzle was still falling from the leaden overcast above, and most people were huddled under umbrellas. Mrs. Larrabee was circulating among them, trying to persuade everyone to take down their umbrellas and join in the dance. Meanwhile, Abner Larrabee, with the help of a couple of other henpecked men, was trying to coax a sodden mass of newspapers and twigs into flame.

The Daughters of Pocahontas had been using this clearing as a meeting place for years, and they had arranged a lot of fieldstones in a circle for seats. At one side of the circle was a sort of gateway where you were supposed to stop and pick up a twig to throw on the council fire in the center as you entered the sacred circle. At the side opposite the gateway was a large slate slab, suspended across two rocks, which served as a kind of throne for whomever was the high muckety-muck of the council. In the center was a ring of smaller stones to mark the spot for the council fire, and this is where Abner Larrabee was striving to get a blaze started.

We clambered up onto the top of Lookout Rock, which was directly behind the throne, to watch the proceedings—all except Dinky Poore, that is. He curled up at the base of the rock in a poncho and fell fast asleep.

A lot of "How! How!"s went up from the women when the first flicker of flame shot up through the stack of kindling Abner was fanning. Raincoats came off, and somebody started beating a drum, and all of a sudden there were about three dozen Indians inside the sacred circle in full regalia. The crowd of onlookers pressed in closer, and before we could even start laughing, Mrs. Larrabee was reciting a mystic chant in some language we couldn't even understand. She was standing in front of the throne with her face turned up to the sky and her arms thrust out to her sides with the palms facing forward, toward the east. A rhythmic clapping from those seated in the circle punctuated her chant, and every once in a while they threw in another "How! How!"

Pretty soon the men in the group stood up and started stamping their feet in time to the clapping. The beat got faster and faster, and soon the chant turned into a song, which everybody was singing. Mrs. Larrabee stepped forward to the council fire, where she raised her arms up high and pointed her fingers toward the sky, and one of the Indian braves leaped out with a large hoop in his hands and started gyrating wildly about the circle, doing all sorts of fancy stunts with the hoop. Then all the braves moved in to form a ring around the fire and started to dance in a circle, stamping their feet hard on the ground and throwing their heads back every time they said, "How!" The women all joined hands and started moving in a larger circle in the opposite direction.

Henry sat on the rock with his chin propped on his knees and stared at the dancers. "Not very scientific!" he said.

Suddenly someone screamed and all the men started beating on the fringes of Mrs. Larrabee's Indian dress, which had caught fire from being too close to the flames. But the dance went on without interruption, in an ever-increasing cadence, and nobody seemed to notice that it had stopped raining.

"Holy mackerel! There's the sun!" shouted Freddy Muldoon, standing up on the rock and pointing across the valley. We all jerked our heads around, and sure enough you could see the top of it shining through a rift in the clouds on the eastern horizon. Mrs. Larrabee heard the shout and brought her head down out of the clouds. She shouted, too, and stretched her arms out straight toward the east. The song changed to an even weirder tune, and all the dancers flung themselves about the circle in wild abandon. Then the dance stopped suddenly, and they all knelt down and bowed toward the east, placing the palms of their hands flat on the ground.

There was a lot of cheering and back-slapping among the spectators, and Mayor Scragg stepped forward with the members of the town council and shook Mrs. Larrabee's hand. The full light of the sun had broken through the rift in the clouds now, and it shone on the faces of the dancers, which were all smeared with some kind of reddish-brown paint.

"I hope I never get old enough to dress up like that!" said Mortimer Dalrymple.

We clambered down off the rock and joined the line of people moving down the path toward the road. We passed right by Mrs. Larrabee, who was still being congratulated by the council members.

"How, Big Chief!" she called out to Henry. "What did you think of the dance?"

"Very nice!" said Henry politely. "You sure picked a good day for it!"

We woke up Dinky Poore and went on down the hill,

muddy and tired, and a little bewildered. It looked as though it would be a nice day.

"I guess you were right again, Henry," said Freddy Muldoon. "Science doesn't know all the answers."

"Neither does Mrs. Larrabee!" said Henry.

The Flying Sorcerer

Dinky Poore didn't usually miss meetings of the Mad Scientists' Club; so, when we hadn't seen him around the clubhouse for four straight days, we figured something was wrong.

"Maybe he deserted, and joined up with Harmon's gang," said Freddy Muldoon, who was probably Dinky's best friend. "He was pretty gloomy all last week, and he hardly opened his mouth."

"Stow it!" said Mortimer Dalrymple. "Dinky wouldn't do that."

"I dunno," Freddy persisted. "He was acting kinda cagey, like, and I haven't laid eyes on him all this week."

"Have you been to his house?" Henry Mulligan asked him.

"Yeah! But he don't answer. I holler through the back fence, like always, and Mrs. Poore says he ain't there. I think he deserted."

"Baloney!" said Homer Snodgrass. "You always want to make a big mystery out of everything."

"Well, I ain't no Pollyanna, like you!" Freddy blustered.

"Go soak your head!" Homer retorted, as Jeff Crocker rapped his gavel on the packing crate and called for order.

"What do you think, Charlie?" Jeff asked me. "You always know what to do with Dinky when he has one of his moods."

"Maybe we could send a delegation around to his house, and find out what's wrong," I suggested. "Or is that too practical?"

"Seems like the least we could do," Mortimer observed. "After all, he might be dead."

"Hoh, Boy!" Freddy snorted, slapping his palm to his forehead. "I hope you never donate your brain to science. It would set civilization back fifty years."

The upshot was that Jeff appointed Freddy and me as a committee of two to make a formal call at Dinky's house. We went there right after the meeting.

"Is Dinky sick?" I asked Mrs. Poore, when she answered the door.

Mrs. Poore looked startled for a moment. Then she said, "Maybe he is! I hadn't thought of that."

"What do you mean?" I asked.

"Well, I don't know, exactly," she said, "but he's been acting strangely, lately. He gets up early, and I pack him a lunch, and I don't see him again until suppertime—or sometimes until 'way after dark. What has he been doing?"

"That's what we wanted to ask *you*," said Freddy.

"Ask *me?*" Mrs. Poore looked startled again. "Why? Hasn't he been with you?"

"We haven't seen Dinky all week," I explained.

"Oh, dear!" said Mrs. Poore, holding the tips of her fingers to her lips. "Don't tell me—No!—I never thought of that!"

Freddy Muldoon screwed his eyes up into tiny slits. "He isn't dead, is he?"

"Oh! Gracious no!" Mrs. Poore laughed. "Whatever gave you that idea, Freddy?"

"Just a nutty friend of mine," Freddy shrugged. "Forget it!"

"Well, do you know where he is, now?" I asked her.

"I've no idea," she said, putting her fingers to her lips again. "I just assumed he'd been with you boys all week. You know how it is..." She hesitated for a moment. "Well, you boys are always busy with some kind of a crazy project—I mean—well, I just don't worry about Dinky, even if he comes in long after midnight, because I know he's working on something important with all of you, and..."

"Never mind, Mrs. Poore. We'll find out what he's up to!" Freddy interrupted her. He gave an exaggerated bow and strode off the porch with me following him.

We knew we could find out where Dinky was, and what he was doing. It was just a question of how long it would take. Unless Dinky had discovered some new hideout that none of us knew about, it was just a matter of checking all our regular haunts until we found him. Jeff ticked off the spots on our big wall map of Mammoth County in his barn: Indian Hill, Brake Hill, Memorial Point, the old zinc mine, the quarry, Mammoth Falls, the old mill on Lemon Creek, Zeke Boniface's junkyard, the old Harkness mansion, Elmer Pridgin's cabin, Jason Barnaby's apple orchard, and a dozen other places. Then he split us up into two-man teams (in the Mad Scientists' Club nobody goes off on a mission alone), and we set off on our bicycles to look for Dinky.

Freddy and I had already checked out Zeke's junkyard, and were heading for the apple orchard when we got a call on the radio from Mortimer. He and Homer claimed they could see Dinky, crouched on top of Lookout Rock high up on Indian Hill. They had hollered to him from the road, but he wouldn't answer their call and they were going up after him.

All of us made for Indian Hill, and when we had scrambled to the summit we found Mortimer and Homer trying to coax Dinky down off the rock. But he wouldn't budge. He just kept scanning the horizon through a pair of binoculars and muttering to himself.

"What's the matter with you, you little nut?" Jeff shouted at him, when he and Henry had arrived. "Come on down here, or we'll come up and get you."

"Go away!" said Dinky petulantly.

"I'm going to count to ten," Jeff warned, "and if you aren't down here I'm coming up to get you."

"Come ahead!" Dinky pouted. "I'll kick anybody in

the face that sticks his head up here."

We all looked at each other. Dinky was peering intently at the horizon.

"Let him stay there 'til he grows up!" Mortimer said, disgustedly.

"If you don't come down, we'll vote you out of the club! How do you like that?" taunted Freddy.

"Yeah!" Mortimer chimed in. "We already voted you 'most likely to secede'. How do you like that?"

"Very funny!" Dinky said with a yawn.

"Dinky, won't you please tell us what you're doing up there?" Henry pleaded.

Dinky pulled his eyes away from the binoculars and stared at Henry for a moment. "I'm looking for flying saucers," he said, matter-of-factly.

Everybody laughed.

"Come on, Dinky. Be serious," Jeff prodded.

"I'm looking for flying saucers!" Dinky repeated.

"How many have you seen?" asked Mortimer.

"I ain't seen none yet," Dinky replied. "But I will."

Everybody laughed again. Then Dinky turned his back on us; but not before we saw a big tear trickle down his left cheek.

"The kid's daft," said Mortimer. "He really means it."

"Look! He's cryin'. He's cryin'," shouted Freddy, jumping up and down.

"Shut up! You big fathead!" Dinky blubbered, throwing down a handful of loose pebbles.

"Wait a minute! Wait a minute!" Henry cautioned. "Let's not get emotional about it. Dinky, if you stay up there in that hot sun much longer you'll see flying saucers alright—and pink elephants, too."

"I don't care," Dinky sniffled. "I'm gonna stay here 'til I see one."

"There ain't no such thing as flying saucers, you nut!" said Freddy Muldoon.

"Yes there is," Dinky persisted. "You read about them in the paper every day. People are seeing them all over the country—everybody except me. I bet I'm the only person in the whole world that hasn't seen one."

"Cool it, man," said Mortimer. "Flying saucers aren't news anymore. They're as old as the hills."

"Nuts to you," said Dinky. "They're the latest."

"Oh, yeah? I just betcha people been seein' them things for three thousand years," Mortimer teased. "I betcha that Arabian that invented the Magic Carpet started the whole thing. I been told people called him the first Flying Sorcerer."

Another handful of pebbles came flying down from the rock, and Henry pulled Mortimer off to one side to talk with Jeff. They whispered together for a minute, and Jeff and Mortimer nodded their heads.

"Dinky!" said Henry, walking back to the base of the rock. "Will you come down if we promise you that we'll build a flying saucer—a real one—just for you?"

"Honest Injun?" said Dinky, doubtfully.

"Honest Injun!"

"Scout's Honor?"

"Scout's Honor!" said Henry.

"A real flying saucer that will fly?"

"A real flying saucer that will fly!" said Henry.

"That's what I thought you'd do!" said Dinky, and he

slid down off the rock.

Henry was true to his word. He had us all working like beavers for the next two weeks, building something far better than anything we had dreamed of. Most of us had thought he was kidding when he told Dinky we would build a flying saucer that could really fly. But when we found out what he had in mind, we got pretty excited.

Henry and Jeff drew up some plans for a real monster of a saucer. It was about twenty feet in diameter and six feet high; shaped like a flat top, or one of those striped Christmas tree ornaments squashed down. Henry explained that we would have to build it on the principle of a dirigible, with a rigid, but very lightweight frame, covered with an envelope of balloon silk. Filled with some of the helium we had left over from our last balloon expedition, it would have enough lift to stay aloft with the added weight of a propulsion system and a few other gadgets Henry had dreamed up to make the experiment more interesting.

We decided to build the thing in one of the old ore car sheds near the entrance to the abandoned zinc mine up in the hills west of Strawberry Lake. Nobody except us ever snooped around there, and besides, Henry figured it would be a good place to operate from once we got the saucer built.

We had most everything we needed, except material for the frame. Henry figured that bamboo would be the best thing, because it is tough and light and easy to work with. But bamboo doesn't grow in our part of the country.

"I know where there's plenty of bamboo," said Freddy Muldoon.

"Where?" asked Jeff.

"I seen a whole load of new fishin' poles—great big ones—comin' in at Snodgrass's Hardware Store."

Everybody turned and looked at Homer. Homer rubbed his nose and dug the toe of one shoe into the top of the other. "Okay!" he said. "I'll volunteer to work in the store Saturday morning."

That solved our problem on the bamboo. Saturday morning Dinky and I sat in the shade in the alley back of Snodgrass's Hardware Store, along with Freddy Muldoon. Every time Homer had an excuse to go back to the stockroom to fill an order, he'd throw another fishing pole out the window, and one of us would lug it down the alley to a vacant lot where we hid them in the tall grass. Homer had to work a little overtime, because it took us until two o'clock in the afternoon before we thought we had enough poles to do the job. Homer's dad was so proud of him for working past noontime that he paid him an extra fifty cents.

With the bamboo poles we constructed two geodesic domes, twenty feet across, and then mated the two together to form a flattened sphere. On top we added a little, flat, circular structure that looked like a tank turret. Henry explained that the geodesic construction, with mutually supporting triangles of bamboo lashed together, would give us the strongest frame with the least amount of material. We didn't need a lot of supporting braces inside, and could use the rest of our bamboo for mounting the propulsion system and the other gadgets we wanted to have on board.

The propulsion system consisted of two large tanks of pressurized carbon dioxide attached to nozzles which protruded from the underside of the saucer. There were two sets of nozzles: one set projecting horizontally, and the other two pointing down at about a forty-five degree angle. With two solenoid-operated valves for each tank, controlled from a central relay box, we could exhaust spurts of carbon dioxide gas through either set of nozzles as a pair, or actuate them individually in any combination we wanted to. In this way we could make the saucer fly straight ahead, zoom upward at a sharp angle, or execute a few banks and turns.

"We'll only be able to fly it when it's fairly calm," Henry said, "because we won't have enough power to buck a strong wind, and we'll run out of fuel pretty fast."

We mounted a bright green light in the turret, and over it we fitted an aluminum cylinder with a slit in it. A little electric motor, powered by a dry cell, would rotate the cylinder just like the reflector for a lighthouse beacon. We installed a ring of clear plexiglass inside the turret, and cemented it to the balloon silk that covered the turret. Then we cut windows through the silk, and we had a first class spook effect that would make anyone think the saucer was sending out coded signals.

Around the perimeter of the saucer we mounted twelve spin rockets that burned a mixture of zinc and sulphur. We could fire any of these by sending a signal through the command receiver, and make the saucer spin on its vertical axis. If we wanted to fire them all at once, we could really create a sensation.

Besides the command receiver, we installed a second receiver for a voice channel and mounted two speakers in the bottom of the saucer—"just in case we want to broadcast messages to Earthlings," Jeff explained.

"Once we get this thing up in the air, how do we get it down again?" asked Freddy Muldoon.

"Good question!" said Mortimer. "That shows you're thinking."

"When I want an answer from you, I'll ask a more stupid question," Freddy retorted.

"It so happens that *is* a very good question, Freddy," Henry interrupted. "Because we're going to have to depend on a good deal of luck to get the thing back down and we may lose it entirely. When and where we try to fly it will depend a lot on wind conditions. What I hope to do is launch it from here, give it a little push from the propulsion tanks, and let it drift out over the lake toward town. It should drift at about a thousand feet. The zinc mine, here, is about five hundred feet above the elevation of the town; so we'd have to try and bring it down, gradually, by letting some of the helium escape as we head it back in this direction."

"Pretty hairy!" said Freddy, scratching his head.

"And that's not all of the problem," said Henry. "We want to make it do a few stunts while it's floating over town; but we have to make sure we have enough carbon dioxide left in the tanks to push it back here. We can save fuel if we have a light wind blowing toward town, or if we have a wind blowing back in this direction. But if we have a crosswind, we just won't be able to fly it."

"Why not let Freddy ride in it?" Mortimer suggested. "He has a lot of extra wind."

Henry ignored the comment, and Freddy curled his lip in disdain.

"Then there's the problem of capturing the thing when it gets back here," Henry continued. "We might have to chase it all over the hillside, even if we get it back down to the right altitude; and it might get fouled up in the trees. It might even miss this ridge of hills and keep on going toward Claiborne."

"If that happens, we could let all the helium out through the escape valve and let it crash wherever it wants to," said Jeff. "We could probably get to it before anyone else could, because we'd know about where it is."

"Seems to me they bring dirigibles down with handlines that they drop over the side. Why don't we do something like that?" I suggested.

"We'll have to," said Henry. "I guess we could coil a couple of ropes on the underside of the saucer, and cut 'em loose with the same command signal that opens the helium escape valve."

"We'll stand a better chance of snatching it if we weight the ropes with some grappling hooks, and string a few hundred yards of wire between the trees up on the ridge, there," said Jeff.

"Now everybody's thinking," said Mortimer.

"Yeah! Everybody but you," sneered Freddy Muldoon.

"I've been thinking, too," said Mortimer, "and I've

thought up a name for this flat balloon. I move we christen it 'The Flying Sorcerer' as a tribute to my wit."

"I like 'The Flat Balloon' better," said Freddy.

"It's my saucer," said Dinky Poore, "and I vote for 'The Flying Sorcerer', because it sounds a lot cornier."

And that was it. We painted the name around the turret, and The Flying Sorcerer was ready to confound the populace of Mammoth Falls.

For the Sorcerer's first voyage we picked a quiet evening when there was scarcely any wind at all. It was dusk, and a few puffy white clouds, high in the sky, reflected the last rays of the sun as the saucer lifted off from the old zinc mine and started to drift toward town. We didn't dare fly the thing in full daylight for fear it would look too phony.

Homer and I were stationed in the loft over his father's hardware store where we could get a good view of the town square. Henry tends to be very scientific about things, even when we're just pulling a prank; so he insisted we take notes of people's reactions in a log book. He figured our observations might provide some valuable psychological data for the people who have to investigate flying saucer reports. While I kept watch at the window, Homer sat cross-legged on the floor and took down everything I described.

7:48 pm: I can just barely see the thing against that bright spot in the clouds. I can't see any lights, so they must not have turned on the beacon yet. It seems to be moving this way, all right. Hey! It looks pretty good.

7:57 pm: There's a man with a straw hat down in the square. I think he sees it. He's scratching his head.

Now he just grabbed another man and he's pointing up in the sky. The beacon light just went on. You can see it flashing around. It looks real weird. Now there's a few people coming out of the Midtown Grill. One man's got a hamburger in his hand. He just dropped it in the street. There comes Billy Dahr down the steps of the police station. No, he's running back inside. The saucer's just about over the square now. It's just hanging up there. Here comes Billy Dahr again. He just forgot

his hat.

Just then Henry called on the radio. He wanted to know if we could see the saucer. "Yes!" said Homer. "A lot of people in the square have already seen it. Better get it out of here."

"We'll give 'em a little show, first," said Henry. "Keep your eyes peeled."

8:00 pm: I think Henry just ignited a couple of the spin rockets. There are a lot of sparks flying out around it. Yeah! It looks like a 4th of July pinwheel up there. Now it's zooming straight up in a spiral. He must have cut in the lift jets. I think Billy Dahr's trying to pick it up in a pair of field glasses. He's holding something up to his eyes. Now he's backing up to get a better view. There's a whole bunch of people around him. Oops! He fell flat on his back in that petunia bed behind the bandstand. I don't think the saucer's spinning any more. Tell Henry to shut off the beacon light! I can just barely see the thing, now. I think it's heading back over the lake.

8:15 pm: There are still a lot of people in the square. They're walking around talking to each other and pointing up in the sky and rubbernecking all over the place. Some of them will probably stay here all night, hoping to see the thing again.

And that was the end of the first report on The Flying Sorcerer's appearance over Mammoth Falls. The rest of the gang back at the zinc mine managed to recapture it, but only after a pretty hairy chase all over the top of the ridge. As far as the people in town were concerned, the saucer just went out of sight when Henry shut the beacon light off. But he had to turn it on again while the thing was still over Strawberry Lake, so he could tell how to maneuver the craft back to the mine. The main trouble was he couldn't tell what direction the nozzles were pointing when he'd give a signal for another squirt of carbon dioxide, and sometimes he'd just push it farther off course. Fortunately a light breeze came up out of the east, and the saucer eventually floated toward the mine of its own accord. It got caught in a slight updraft just as it reached the hills, and though Henry let a lot of the helium escape in a hurry, the thing just kept bobbing up and down in the updraft and almost popped over the ridge. Just when they thought they had lost it, one of the grappling hooks caught in the topmost branches of a tall ash and Dinky shinnied up to tie a line to it.

We decided we wouldn't fly the saucer again until we had added a rudder over the point where the propulsion nozzles projected from the underside of the body. This would give it more directional stability, and also tell us what direction the nozzles were pointing.

The next day the Mammoth Falls *Gazette* had the story plastered all over its front page. MYSTERIOUS OBJECT SEEN IN SKY. MANY RESIDENTS TELL OF SIGHTING FLYING SAUCER. CONSTABLE DAHR GIVES EYEWITNESS DESCRIPTION OF STRANGE CRAFT. AIR FORCE PROMISES INVESTIGATION. Freddy Muldoon brought some copies to the clubhouse so we could cut out the articles to keep our scrapbook up to date, and Mortimer Dalrymple read them all out loud. They were pretty wild.

One man claimed the saucer had zoomed off at five thousand miles an hour when it went out of sight. When a reporter asked him how he could tell it was moving that fast, he said, "I'm a good judge of speed!" Another man said the thing was about the size of a house, and it would zoom up to twenty-thousand feet and then come back down again as though it was looking for a place to land. Several people said that if you looked straight at the thing it made you feel dizzy, and one man said he was blinded for about five minutes by an intense beam of light that zapped him right in the eyes. A woman swore she saw a man jump out of the craft and parachute down to earth, but nobody else would agree with her. There were many reports of a loud humming noise coming from the saucer, and some people commented on a strange smell in the air.

"Hey! That smell's not a bad idea," said Mortimer. "Let's drop a load of stink bombs next time."

"Maybe we could make the thing cackle and lay a few rotten eggs," mused Freddy.

Even Henry laughed at the possibilities this suggested. "That's something to think about," he admitted, "but it's too early for stunts like that. We don't want to tip our hand yet."

The next day's paper carried an interview with Colonel March, the commander at Westport Field. The colonel said he had made a full report on the Mammoth Falls "incident" to the Project Blue Book office at Wright-Patterson Field in Ohio. "It is their job to investigate all reports of unidentified flying objects," he told the *Gazette*, "and they have promised to send a team of investigators here immediately."

The investigators, headed by a professor of psychology from Columbia University, showed up that very day, in fact. But they were very secretive about their investigation. They wouldn't make any statements for publication, except to say that there was nothing unusual about the "Mammoth Falls sightings," as far as they could tell. One member of the team, a professor of physics, said that meteorological records showed there had been a temperature inversion in the Mammoth Falls area the day the phenomenon was seen, and that "aerial mirages are not uncommon under such conditions." This explanation, of course, satisfied no one.

The team spent three days in town interviewing eyewitnesses; many of whom, we were sure, hadn't seen anything at all. The day after they left town we flew The Flying Sorcerer again.

On its second voyage the saucer performed well, and Mortimer broadcast some weird sound effects over the speakers to satisfy those people who had thought they heard a loud humming noise coming from the craft. But as soon as the thing was sighted somebody called the Air Force at Westport Field to report it. The Air Force claimed there was nothing on their radar, but after they had several calls they agreed to scramble two chase planes to investigate.

We didn't know what was going on, of course, but we did hear the jets screaming overhead as they passed over town on their takeoff. We guessed what it meant, and Homer called Henry on the radio in time to get the beacon light on the saucer turned off before the planes could circle back on their search pattern. Henry headed the craft for the hills at full thrust. From the zinc mine he could see the two jets catch the last rays of the sun as they banked to return and he figured there wouldn't be time to get The Flying Sorcerer back to the hills before they would sight it. But darkness was closing in fast, and there might be a chance if he could bring it in low over the lake where it was almost as dark as night.

The idea was a good one, but in his excitement Henry let too much helium escape and The Flying Sorcerer plopped into the lake before it reached the far shore, with its carbon dioxide fuel exhausted. It floated like a cork, though, and when we managed to make our way through the dense woods on the western shore a couple of hours later, we found it sitting like a duck on a pond about two hundred yards out in the lake. Jeff and Mortimer swam out and took it in tow, and when they brought it to shore we nudged it into one of the deep coves that reach back among the fingers of the hills in that area. We camouflaged it as well as we could with branches and leaves, and left it there until we could figure out how to get it back in the air again.

What we didn't know at the time was that the pilot of one of the chase planes had caught sight of it just before it settled into the murky shadows below the horizon, and had managed to train his gun cameras on it. The pilot figured he had the first picture of a flying saucer ever taken by an Air Force plane, and the Information Officer at Westport Field lost no time in getting the photo spread across the front page of the *Gazette* the next morning.

If we thought we were causing a stir before, it was nothing compared to what happened now. Colonel March didn't have to request an investigation this time. All sorts of amateur "investigators" of flying saucers and psychic phenomena descended on Mammoth Falls, and the Project Blue Book officials set up a field office in the Town Hall. The pilot who took the picture found himself taking lie detector tests. Then he was sent to Wright-Patterson Air Force Base for a mental examination, so none of the amateur investigators or the press could talk to him. Lieutenant Graham, the Information Officer, got bawled out for releasing the picture to the newspaper before the Air Force could authenticate it. Colonel March found himself right in the middle. He was being harassed by reporters for a statement, and the Pentagon was telling him to keep his mouth shut.

Nobody knew what had happened to the saucer after the pilot lost sight of it, and rumors were flying around town that the thing had crashed in the hills and little green men had been seen trying to thumb rides from motorists. There was scarcely anybody on the streets after dark, and Lem Perkins refused to make milk deliveries until after the sun came up. There was a regular panic among housewives when some dolt started a rumor that all the hens in the area were laying radioactive eggs, and Mayor Scragg had to ask the Department of Agriculture to test all the eggs in the stores. Effajean Lightbody, who is president of the Mammoth Falls Woman's Club, wrote a letter to the *Gazette* asking the mayor to put a curfew into effect after eight P.M.; and Abner Sharples, who wants to be mayor, told the Lions Club that if he was running the town he'd ask the governor to send in the National Guard so people could sleep at night.

During the daytime a lot of adventurous volunteers were scouring the hills west of Strawberry Lake, hoping to find a crew of Martian astronauts waiting for an invitation to the White House, but nobody found anything. Harmon Muldoon, Freddy's cousin, led a group of searchers to the old zinc mine; but we had moved all our radio gear out of there, and the place looked as abandoned as ever. We figured we'd just lay low for a while and let human nature take its course. It did, the very next day.

Freddy and I were helping Henry mow his back lawn when Mrs. Mulligan called from the kitchen door to say Henry had an important visitor. She acted all flustered and excited.

"I'll bet I know who that is," Henry said with a nervous little laugh. "You guys better come in with me."

We went inside to find Colonel March sitting in the big Boston rocker in Mrs. Mulligan's living room. He looked pretty haggard and his uniform was a little crumpled, but he was just as cheerful as ever. Mrs. Mulligan was darting about the room picking up papers and wiping the dust off things with her apron. "Excuse me," she said, "I'll just be a minute!" And with that she swept a handful of peanut shells off an end table into her apron pocket and disappeared into the kitchen.

"I was just driving by and thought I'd drop in and say 'hello'," said the colonel as he got up to shake hands.

"Hello!" said Henry.

"You won't be able to drive much farther," said Freddy Muldoon. "This is a dead end street."

The colonel chuckled indulgently and tweaked Freddy's left ear as he settled back into his seat. Then he looked straight at Henry and said, very casually, "What have you been up to, lately?"

"Nothing much," said Henry.

"Nothing much?"

"The same old stuff," Henry shrugged.

The colonel fished in his pocket for a cigarette. "What do you think of all the excitement in town?" he asked.

"What excitement?" said Freddy Muldoon.

The colonel chuckled again and lit his cigarette. "I mean all this business about flying saucers," he explained.

"Oh, that! Some people are real kooks!" said Freddy.

"What do you think, Henry?"

"I think it's very amusing," said Henry, rubbing his nose.

"Yes, I suppose it is amusing," the colonel agreed, "but I haven't been able to get any sleep for three nights in a row, now."

"That's too bad," said Henry, clasping his hands over one knee.

The conversation lapsed and the colonel stared at the ceiling for a while. Then he shifted uneasily in his seat and started to twirl his hat between his knees. Finally, he cleared his throat and said, "I was thinking you boys might be able to help me out."

"We're not much good on insomnia," said Henry.

"Why don't you go see a doctor?" suggested Freddy.

The colonel laughed again, a little bitterly. "I don't think I need a doctor," he said. "But if we could cut this investigation short, I might be able to get some sleep."

There was another silence. In the middle of it Mrs. Mulligan came bustling in with a cup of tea for Colonel March and a plate of cucumber sandwiches. "Won't you have a cup of tea, Colonel March? It will do you good," she said. "You must be a very busy man just now. My, isn't this flying saucer business a caution, though. Excuse me, I must get my wash out on the line." And she disappeared into the kitchen again.

The colonel smiled his appreciation, but looked askance at the sandwiches. "Cucumber sandwiches?" he said, uncertainly.

"Yes! They're very good," said Henry.

"Have one," said Freddy, taking a handful. "They make you burp."

"I might try just one," said the colonel. "I haven't had time for any lunch today." He took one sandwich and munched it speculatively. Then he fastened his light blue eyes directly on me.

"To get back to what we were discussing," he said, "have any of you boys seen any flying saucers around here?"

I looked at Freddy, and Freddy looked at Henry, and Henry uncrossed his legs and clasped his hands around the other knee. "What do you mean by a flying saucer, Colonel?" he asked.

"Well, let's just say any strange object in the sky that you can't explain."

"No!" said Henry. I breathed a little easier and Freddy reached for another handful of sandwiches.

The colonel popped the rest of his sandwich into his mouth and chewed it thoughtfully. "That's too bad!" he said. "I just hoped you boys might have some valuable information for me."

Freddy gurgled something unintelligible through a mouthful of sliced cucumber.

"Yes, I certainly agree!" said the colonel. "You were right, Henry. Those sandwiches are awfully good. I think I'll just have another." But his hand stopped in mid-air as he saw that the plate was already empty.

"You have to move fast when you're at the same table with Freddy," said Henry. "Let me get you another one from the kitchen."

"Oh, no! Thank you," said the colonel. "I think I'd better be getting on now, anyway." And he picked up his hat and strode to the door.

"Whew!" I whistled when the colonel had gone. "Maybe we'd better lay low for awhile."

"You told a lie!" said Freddy Muldoon, pointing a stubby finger at Henry.

"No, I didn't," Henry protested. "He asked me if I had seen anything in the sky that I couldn't explain, and I said 'No,' and that's the truth."

Freddy thought this over for awhile. "Boy, you ought to be a politician when you grow up!" he said, finally.

"If you ever run for President, remind me to vote for somebody else."

"I still think we ought to lay low for awhile," I repeated.

"I don't know about that," Henry said. "That's just what they'd expect us to do. If Colonel March really suspects us, and I think he does, then we'd be tipping our hand by knocking off operations. He'd figure he had the problem solved, and that he guessed right. If we really want to obfuscate everybody, the thing we should do is launch The Flying Sorcerer as soon as we can—tonight. Nobody would think we'd have the nerve to do that right after Colonel March came to see us."

"Hey! You just used a forty-eight-cent word," said Freddy. "How do we *obscufate* everybody?"

"That's *obfuscate!*" said Henry. "Let's just say it means we keep 'em guessing."

Since Harmon Muldoon had led the Project Blue Book investigators to our operations center at the old zinc mine, we decided we had to become more mobile. What we needed was a big truck to mount all our equipment in, so we could move around from place to place. Zeke Boniface, who runs the most interesting junkyard in town, had just the truck we needed, so we took him into our confidence.

Zeke's truck, Richard The Deep Breather, is an ancient rig, but he always manages to keep it running. Not that anyone else could. There is a mysterious relationship between Zeke and the truck that is hard to explain. You know how some mechanical things will only respond to the tinkering of one person? That's how it is with Richard The Deep Breather. If it weren't for Zeke, the old truck would be part of the huge pile of rusting junk in his yard, instead of the living, deep-breathing monster it is. True mechanical genius is a rare gift, and Zeke has it. He believes in doing things with as little human effort as possible. His junkyard is so full of labor-saving contraptions that he can run the whole operation without ever getting off the broken-down couch in his office, if he wants to. It's a fact that Zeke has enough brains to be a millionaire, except that he'd rather fish.

We mounted all our radio gear in the truck, and Zeke picked up the Sorcerer after we had hauled it from its hiding place in the cove to the Lake Road. He drove it to the zinc mine well before dusk with Henry, Mortimer, and Jeff on board. Homer and I stayed behind to monitor the flight of the Sorcerer from the loft over the Snodgrass hardware store.

Dinky and Freddy had a special assignment. Henry figured it might be the last flight for The Flying Sorcerer, and he wanted Dinky and Freddy to "obfuscate everybody real good," as Freddy put it. The radio news that afternoon had carried an announcement by Colonel March. He said his own investigation had disclosed no evidence of unidentified flying objects in the area, that the sightings which had been reported had a plausible explanation, and that he was sending the Project Blue Book investigators home. In answer to questions, he would only say that he had "solved the mystery" to his own satisfaction, and that he was reasonably certain there would be no more UFO reports coming from the Mammoth Falls area.

Henry had gone into one of his blue funks when he heard the broadcast, and nobody could communicate with him for about fifteen minutes. When he came out of it, he pulled Freddy and Dinky off to one side and gave them some rapid-fire instructions. They scooted out of the clubhouse, where we had been planning the night's operations, and we didn't see them again until evening.

From where we sat in the loft over the hardware store, Homer and I could just barely see the high ridge of the hills beyond Strawberry Lake silhouetted against the fading light of the sunset. In the town square, three stories beneath us, there were the usual late evening strollers and gossips swapping exaggerated accounts of the day's events, and rumors of imagined events. The fire department crew had set their hoses out to dry in front of the station during the afternoon, and they were now busily engaged in folding them back into the racks on the trucks. A four-piece Salvation Army band was playing hymns rather loudly, and a little off-key, in front of Garmisch's Sausage Shop. Nobody was paying any attention to them, except two dogs that always hang around in front of the sausage shop for some reason. They were sitting at the curb, howling every time the coronet player blew a high note.

Suddenly, Homer pinched my arm and pointed toward the far shore of the lake. There were two tiny, bright objects bobbing on the horizon just above the ridge of the hills. Soon, a third one appeared; then another, and another. One of them suddenly zoomed upward, far above the others, and continued soaring in an ever-widening circle, describing a spiral in the half-darkened sky. More of the objects began to appear now, over the same section of the ridge, as though they had flown in from the west. Some of the objects looked like glowing, white lights. Others had a bluish tinge to them.

This was our signal that the night's operation had begun. With Zeke's help, Henry, Mortimer, and Jeff were launching a barrage of "ghost lights," as Henry called them. These were plastic bags with the open end taped to a piece of wire mesh, or a large can lid with holes punched in it. We'd put a can of canned heat, or a large candle inside the bag, cemented to the can lid. The result is the same thing as a hot air balloon, and they'll do crazier things than a kite when the air currents catch them. They'll zoom way up in the air, and then drop down just as suddenly. They'll hover, almost motionless, in one spot for a while; then scoot off sideways for a couple of miles. To people on the ground they look like something that can't happen.

By now there were about two dozen of the ghost lights swirling in crazy patterns over Strawberry Lake—enough to make the most sober citizen swear the town was being invaded by hundreds of flying saucers. And every minute the prevailing wind from the west was blowing them closer to Mammoth Falls. Close on their heels came the familiar flashing green light of The Flying Sorcerer. In another minute the evening strollers in the town square would be able to see them. Homer and I held our breath. Sitting side-by-side at the loft

window, we could feel each other's nerves twitching.

As we watched The Flying Sorcerer draw nearer to town, I switched on the radio to establish contact with Henry. Our plan was that Homer and I would take over control of the Sorcerer once it appeared over town, because we had a rather delicate maneuver in mind. We could get a stronger signal up to the Sorcerer's receiver from the antenna we had mounted on the roof over the loft, and we could exercise better control than we could by relaying instructions to Henry.

The Sorcerer was coming in low—just a few hundred feet above the ground—because it had been weighted down with lead sash weights to keep it well below its normal one-thousand-foot altitude. Consequently, it caught everyone by surprise as it loomed over the roof of the fire station, and hovered there while everybody in the town square was busy watching the antics of the ghost lights. But they noticed it when a loud hissing sound drew their attention. Homer was letting enough helium escape from the Sorcerer to bring it down on the flat, graveled roof of the fire station. When the crowd saw it, it was losing altitude rapidly; and it hit the roof of the fire station with an audible *thunk*, disappearing from the view of those in the square.

The crowd, in a near panic, surged to the other side of the town square; some to try and get a better view, others just trying to get out of the way in case anything happened. Two venturesome young men were trying desperately to shinny up a telephone pole in the hopes of being able to see over the parapet of the fire station roof. The Salvation Army band had stopped playing, and its members were gazing in open-mouthed astonishment at the firemen pouring out of the station house. The two dogs in front of Garmisch's Sausage Shop were howling like coyotes, with their noses thrust up in the air.

What the onlookers couldn't see were the green-costumed figures of Dinky and Freddy, who had been hiding on the roof for two hours, and who had now scrambled over to The Flying Sorcerer to unlash the lead sash weights dangling from the rim of its framework.

When they had the last one cut loose, they waved frantically in our direction, and Homer looked at me with a dumb, blank look on his face.

"That's the signal," I whispered, hoarsely. And when he didn't respond, I poked him a good one in the ribs. "Cut in the jets! Cut in the jets!" I hollered in his ear. Finally Homer came alive as he saw the Sorcerer slowly rising from the roof after being relieved of its added weight. The transmitter buzzed as he sent the signal for all four of the jet nozzles to open up. The Flying Sorcerer zoomed upward with a loud swoosh, bringing a startled shout from the spectators in the square.

The fire station crew had rolled the big hook-and-ladder rig out front, and were starting to raise a ladder to the roof when they heard the noise. Everybody looked up at once to see two green heads with horns, peering back at them over the parapet of the roof. As the crowd gasped, tiny lights on the ends of the horns blinked on and off. Then something approaching pandemonium broke loose as the two green figures clambered onto the top of the parapet and ran back and forth as though they were looking for a way to jump down to the street. One was quite skinny, and the other was quite fat; but both were small.

A group of firemen rushed back into the station house and came running out with a life net. A weird, out-of-this-world pantomime took place for a few moments as the two green figures ran uncertainly from one corner of the station house to the other, and the crew of firemen stumbled back and forth with the life net, trying to keep it beneath them.

Suddenly, the two green figures leaped from the parapet onto the roof again, and disappeared from view. For a moment nothing happened. The crowd was silent, as though they expected the pair to reappear. The firemen were frozen in position, ready to move with the life net, or run the ladder up if the green figures showed themselves again.

But Freddy and Dinky were long gone. They had dropped down through a skylight in the fire station roof, and scrambled to the brass pole leading to the ground floor.

"Me first!" Dinky said, tersely, as he flung himself at the pole, wrapped his arms around it, and slid like greased lightning to the station house floor. "Geronimo!" grunted Freddy, under his breath, as his stomach hit the pole. He hit the floor with a thud, barely missing Dinky, who was scrambling to his feet; and when he flexed his knees to take up the shock, the seat of his pants split wide open. If anyone had been in the fire station at the time, he would have seen a skinny green figure disappearing through the door to the back alley, followed by a fat one with a white bottom.

So fascinated had Homer and I been by the activities in front of the fire station, that we had forgotten all about The Flying Sorcerer. Henry's voice on the radio brought us back to reality.

"You forgot to cut off the jets, Homer," I screamed at him. "The Sorcerer's almost out of sight!"

"Tell Henry to take over control," Homer answered, "he can handle it better than I can."

But when I passed this on to Henry, he said, "I can't.

Uh ...we have company. I guess you'll have to continue the experiment like we planned."

"Like we planned what? Henry, we never planned nothin'. Do you mean you want us to try and get the Sorcerer back to the zinc mine?"

"No... that won't be necessary. Just use your best judgment."

"Henry! Have you gone nuts? This is Charlie, remember?"

"I said we have company!" Henry repeated. "And they're very impressed with our tropospheric scatter experiments."

I decided Henry had gone off his rocker, for sure. But what Homer and I didn't know was that Henry and the others *did* have company. Just about the time the Sorcerer was settling down over the fire station, Colonel March had shown up at the zinc mine with the Project Blue Book investigators. Naturally, they expressed a great deal of interest and curiosity over what the members of the Mad Scientists' Club were doing with all that radio gear set up in Zeke Boniface's truck, just at the time when the sky was full of crazy, whirling lights.

"We're conducting some tropospheric scatter experiments," Henry had explained, when the professor from Columbia inquired about the directional transmitting antenna on the truck. "We set up whenever there are unusual cloud formations in the area and test receptivity at various points around the valley by bouncing signals off the clouds."

"Very interesting, indeed!" observed a neatly

dressed, dark-faced little man, whom Colonel March introduced as Professor Rhama Dhama Rau from the Massachusetts Institute of Technology. "How do you measure signal strength?"

"We haven't gotten around to that," Henry answered, evasively.

It was then he got on the radio to let us know what had happened. I couldn't figure out for sure what Henry was trying to tell me, but I knew something was wrong.

"Listen, Henry, we've got real troubles," I told him. "Homer's lost control of the Sorcerer, because he let all the carbon dioxide escape. It's so far upstairs now that I can barely see the beacon light. It seems to be heading northeast, and I think it's been caught in a jet stream. It's moving pretty fast."

"Yes, I see it!" Henry answered. "I mean…yes, I see. Well…uh…I think that's all we can do for tonight."

"Well, what do you want us to do, Henry?"

There was a confused pause. Then Henry said, rather indefinitely, "You might get on your bikes and meet us at the White Fork Road bridge over Lemon Creek. I think it would do us all good to take a long ride tonight."

I guessed what Henry meant. "When?" I asked.

"Right away!" Henry said.

While Henry had been talking to me on the radio, Mortimer had quietly disappeared from the group clustered around Zeke's truck and had managed to purloin the rotor from the distributor on Colonel March's car. When he returned to the truck, Henry and Jeff were politely shaking hands with the two professors while Zeke coaxed Richard The Deep Breather's balky engine back to life.

"We'll follow behind you to make sure you get home safely!" Colonel March shouted above the engine's deep-throated roar.

"Oh, don't bother!" Jeff shouted back. "You've got more important things to worry about. We'll get home alright."

When Zeke wheeled Richard the Deep Breather across the bridge at the bottom of the ravine below the zinc mine, they could still hear Colonel March grinding the starter on his sedan; and The Flying Sorcerer was the merest speck of light, sailing high and away to the northeast. A strong wind had come up, and the rumble of thunder could be heard off to the southwest.

"Head for Claiborne!" Henry shouted to Zeke while he tried to train the antenna on the fleeing Sorcerer. "We've got about one chance in a thousand of catching her, but we might as well try."

There was real pandemonium in the town square as Homer and I threaded our way through the crowds, heading for the White Fork Road bridge. People seemed to be about evenly divided in their reaction to what had happened. Some were trying to organize search parties to go look for the little green men. Others were trying to pretend that they hadn't seen anything at all. Sirens were wailing, as squad cars from both the police station and the sheriff's office were trying to get out of the square to respond to calls that were coming in from the countryside. We heard somebody say that Henry Applegate had called in and reported two glowing objects that swooped low over his pasture and stampeded his cows. He wanted the police to do something about it, because he knew all his milk was going to be sour in the morning. On one of the police car radios we could hear another patrol car reporting in that he was being chased up the Claiborne Turnpike by a strange blue light that kept diving at his car, and then zooming up into the sky again. The wind was really blowing now, and bending the trees along Chestnut Street. It looked like a whingdinger of a storm was going to hit us, and Homer and I bent over the handlebars of our bicycles and squinted our eyes as we pedaled for dear life to get to the bridge.

Dinky and Freddy were through for the night. After they high-tailed it down the alley behind the fire station, they ducked into a storm drain at the corner and just plain disappeared. We have wonderful storm drains in Mammoth Falls. We get pretty heavy rains in the early spring, and the center of town used to get flooded almost every year. But the town council finally decided to stop messing around with the problem, and they installed a drainage system with six-foot concrete pipe that a man can stand up in. All Freddy and Dinky had to do was stay underground for a few blocks, until they were out of the center of town. Then they could take off their green suits and come up out of the storm drain any place they wanted to. We didn't worry about them.

Some heavy drops of rain had already begun to fall by the time we got to the bridge. When Zeke Boniface finally chugged around the bend in the road with Richard The Deep Breather under a full head of steam, it was coming down in sheets—like somebody was dumping buckets full of the stuff from somewhere in the great upstairs. Zeke had his battered derby pulled down tight over his forehead, and he was rolling the butt of a sodden cigar from side to side in his mouth, even though it had long ago gone out. Homer and I were soaked to the skin, but we handed our bicycles up to Jeff and Mortimer and clambered aboard.

"We're having trouble making contact," Henry shouted above the din of the steady tattoo of rain on the truck's tarpaulin. "But the wind seems to be blowing her straight up the Claiborne Turnpike, and we're heading there now."

"What's happened to Colonel March and those professors?" I asked, after I had time to blow all the water out of my nose.

"They decided to stay up at the zinc mine," said Mortimer.

"The colonel had a little trouble with the engine in his car," Jeff explained. "I'm afraid he's going to miss all the excitement."

Mortimer was monitoring the police net with one radio so he could pass on reports of sightings to Henry. Meanwhile, Jeff wrestled with the tracking antenna every time the road took a sudden turn, trying to keep it pointed in the general direction we thought the

Sorcerer was heading. Henry would raise his hand in the air when he caught the beep of the Sorcerer's beacon on his earphones, and wave left or right to let Jeff know he'd lost it.

"If I can get a steady beep long enough to send a signal through, I'll let most of the helium out and try to bring her down someplace where we can get to her," said Henry.

"I agree with that," said Mortimer. "That's a lot easier than trying to get the truck up to where the saucer is."

Jeff aimed a blow at Mortimer's head, but he had already ducked. "This is no time for jokes. Keep your mind on what you're doing."

"I'll make a note of that!" said Mortimer.

Zeke couldn't go very fast, the way it was raining; but Henry figured we had to be gaining ground on the Sorcerer, because the weather reports said the wind was only twenty-five miles an hour. Two police cars passed us with their lights flashing and their sirens wailing.

"They must be heading for Hiram Poore's place," said Mortimer. "He reported a strange object with a flashing green light sailing over his apple orchard."

"Good!" said Henry. "That gives us some kind of a fix. Tell Zeke to turn off at Indian Hill Road and head for the Prendergast farm. Maybe we can intercept it there."

I told Zeke what to do, and when we had turned onto Indian Hill Road I told him to step on the gas. We were heading for the other side of the ridge of hills that separates the Claiborne Turnpike from Indian Hill

Road. We hoped we could get to the Prendergast farm before the Sorcerer made it over the ridge. As soon as we had gotten around the south end of the ridge and headed north, Henry shot his arm up in the air and practically crowed.

"I've got it! I've got it!" he cried. "A good, steady beep. I'm going to let the helium escape and try to bring her down."

I crawled into the front seat of the truck beside Zeke and stuck my head out over the canvas top of the cab. I couldn't see very far with the rain beating me in the face, but I figured I'd be able to catch sight of the Sorcerer's turret light if it came into view. If I thought I was wet before, it was nothing compared to the soaking I took standing out there on the running board step. The water seemed to be running right through me. The back of my shirt was just as wet as the front. But it was a good thing I was out there. I caught a flicker of light in the corner of my left eye, and I figured it couldn't be anything but the Sorcerer, because the weather was too bad for airplanes, and there just isn't anything else on Indian Hill Ridge but rocks, trees, and grass.

"Bring her down, Henry, bring her down," I gurgled as loud as I could. "There she is! There she is!"

I clung to the handgrip at the side of the windshield and rested my chin on the canvas. With my free hand I shielded my eyes from the rain and strained to catch another glimpse of the Sorcerer. As we rounded the bend where the road crosses Willow Creek, I caught sight of it again. It was plummeting downward across

the face of Indian Hill Ridge. Then, suddenly, it disappeared behind a hillock to our left.

"Turn in at the lane to Prendergast's farm," I shouted to Zeke.

He waved and chomped down harder on the stub of the cigar in his mouth. As he swung Richard The Deep Breather into the rocky dirt road leading to Joel Prendergast's big red farmhouse, the rain suddenly abated. The center of the storm had passed on to the north, and there was just the slightest sprinkle of rain coming down. Then the moon broke through a rift in the clouds and lighted up the sodden pastures on either side of the road. And there was the Sorcerer, drifting aimlessly in the breeze not more than twenty feet off the ground. It drifted right into the side of the Prendergast barn, bumped it twice, and then slid around a corner.

We could see two figures running toward the barn from the rear of the house as the Sorcerer plunged down a steep, grassy slope, heading for a rickety cow shed in the lower meadow. It hit the shed and cows started scattering in all directions. Then we lost sight of the whole spectacle as the lane turned behind a wooded hillock. I jabbed Zeke in the ribs.

"Take that wagon road up to Chestnut Hill," I shouted. "Maybe we can get out in front of her and grab her when she hits the slope. She hasn't got enough lift to get over the hill."

All the guys in the back of the truck had their heads sticking out around the edge of the tarpaulin as we jounced along the wagon road that twisted up the slope of the hill. We were about halfway up when two blasts from what sounded like a shotgun echoed among the sawed-off tree stumps that dotted the crest of the hill.

"Stop here!" I shouted to Zeke, and Richard The Deep Breather shuddered to a full stall as he slammed on the brakes.

We all scrambled out of the truck, clambered through the barbed wire fence that separated the road from the pasture, and headed for a clump of big juniper bushes about twenty yards away. Two more shotgun blasts split the air, and we stuck our heads up above the juniper to see Joel Prendergast puffing and stumbling up the slope of the hill, blasting away at the Sorcerer whenever he could get within range. His wife was farther down the slope with a big stick in her hand, hoping to scare off their huge Holstein bull, who was snorting and pawing the ground, trying to find a way up to where all the excitement was. Their hired hand was floundering around somewhere to the rear of the bull, managing to keep out of the action and still look busy.

We crouched there behind the bush, wanting to dash out and save the Sorcerer, but knowing that we might get a seat full of buckshot if we did. We watched, helpless, as Joel Prendergast unloaded two more barrels and blasted a gaping hole in the side of the craft. The last of the helium escaped with a whoosh, and the once proud Sorcerer came crashing to the ground. You could hear the bamboo struts snapping loose inside her.

Just then the Holstein bull raised his nose in the air and gave out with a bellow that left no doubt of his intention. He pawed the ground twice, snorted loudly, then charged headlong up the slope toward the Sorcerer. Mrs. Prendergast scampered out of the way, and Joel barely made it to safety behind an outcropping of granite as a pair of flashing horns mounted on fourteen hundred pounds of muscle zipped past him and plowed head-on into the fragile silk and bamboo hull. He went right through it, of course, and it collapsed around him. He was still bellowing and thrashing around inside the thing, trying to get his horns loose, when we crawled away from the juniper and made our way back through the pasture fence.

"What a mess!" said Mortimer Dalrymple, after we had gotten through the fence. "If that bull had any sense he'd have known that saucer might be full of little green men with death ray guns, and all that stuff."

"That's what ignorance will do to you," said Henry. "You can't fool anybody who's really stupid."

Dinky Poore was blubbering, like he usually does when one of our projects comes a cropper; but this time it was worse, because he always felt The Flying Sorcerer had been built just for him and he had a very personal attachment to it. Homer Snodgrass tried to comfort him, but Dinky pushed him away.

"Phew! You stink!" he said.

"I do not!" Homer protested.

"Oh, yes you do," said Freddy Muldoon. "You sure don't smell like no rose."

"I must've stepped in something bad!" said Homer, trying to inspect his shoes in the darkness.

"I think you sat in it!" said Mortimer Dalrymple. "Just for that you'll have to ride on the running board.

You're not getting in the back of the truck with me."

"Me, neither!" said Freddy Muldoon.

So Homer rode home standing up on the running board, while the rest of us stretched out in the back of Richard The Deep Breather and dreamed about real flying saucers and imaginary bulls.

The Great Confrontation

It was war! Total war! Harmon Muldoon's gang had invaded practically every secret haunt of The Mad Scientists' Club.

We didn't mind so much when they started using the council ring on Indian Hill for their so-called secret meetings, because we could spy on them whenever we wanted to. And we really didn't care about them trying to rig up the old Harkness mansion with a lot of hoked-up gimmicks that were supposed to scare people. We had already gotten our laughs out of that one, and we knew that nobody in town really believed the place was haunted.

"They're just a buncha cheap copycats!" Dinky Poore had sneered, when we first heard about what they were doing.

But we began to get worried when we discovered they had taken the rusty old handcar out of the zinc mine and dumped it into the river where the big bend curves eastward about eight miles down the track. And finally, we knew they were bent on deliberate harassment when they raided our clubhouse in Jeff Crocker's barn early one Saturday morning and kidnapped Dinky and Harmon's cousin, Freddy Muldoon.

Jeff was the first one to learn of it, when he went out to the barn to do some work on a chemistry experiment he and Henry Mulligan were smelling the place up with. He didn't exactly find a ransom note, but you could call it the same thing. It was a message Harmon Muldoon had taped on one of our recorders, and then tapped into the circuit for opening our clubhouse door. The volume was turned on full blast.

To get into our clubhouse you have to know the diabolical system Henry Mulligan devised for springing the lock. First, you have to know where the photoelectric beam is located, and then you have to trigger it by intercepting the beam with your hand in the proper code sequence. Henry could set it up for any combination of Morse code signals, but this particular week we were using the SOS signal (...−−−...). For a dash, you held your hand in the beam for almost a full second. For a dot, you just flicked it through the beam as fast as you could. After you had given the proper code signal, you could hear the lock snap, and then you could push the door open.

But instead of the lock snapping open when Jeff triggered the beam, all he heard was the loud raspberry that Harmon Muldoon opened his message with:

> "PFFFFFFFFFFRRRRRRMMMMPPPPH! IF YOU WANT TO KNOW WHERE DINKY AND FREDDY ARE, YOU'LL HAVE TO GIVE US THE MIDGET SUBMARINE AND THE RIGHT TO USE THE COOL CAVERN. MAKE UP YOUR MINDS, CHUMS, 'CAUSE FREDDY WON'T HAVE NOTHING TO EAT WHERE HE'S GOING. LEAVE YOUR ANSWER UNDER A ROCK BEHIND THE CANNON AT MEMORIAL POINT."

Jeff kicked the door open, which wasn't locked at all, and hooked up the tape recorder properly again, so he could re-run the tape. There were two things Harmon Muldoon didn't understand, he figured. One was that the Cool Cavern had been blocked off ever since a big piece of the ledge had broken off Mammoth Falls, and the only way to get in there was through the underwater passage. The other thing was that Freddy Muldoon never went anywhere without two baloney sandwiches hidden somewhere in his clothing. He'd even been known to keep one in his shoe. This made a pretty flat sandwich, but with Freddy it was the calories that counted.

Jeff sat for a long while on Henry Mulligan's old piano stool with the heel of one hand propped under his chin, just thinking. Every time he shifted position and spun the seat of the stool around, he made a mental note to tell Henry to oil the thing. It squeaked like the lid of a used coffin.

Finally, Jeff got up off the stool and threw the switch that activates the panic buzzer in the house of every member of the Mad Scientists' Club. As president, Jeff Crocker has authority to call an emergency meeting without pushing the panic button, like the rest of us have to; but this time he felt it was important to get us all together as fast as possible.

While the members of the Mad Scientists' Club were scrambling onto their bicycles to head for Jeff Crocker's barn, Dinky and Freddy were standing on the shore of a small island way out in Strawberry Lake, shouting insults at a retreating rowboat. Harmon Muldoon and Stony Martin were thumbing their noses at the two figures on the shore from the rear seat of the

boat, while Buzzy McCauliffe pulled a steady oar toward a cove in the northwest corner of the lake. Dinky and Freddy were still hurling abuses into the wind when the rowboat disappeared around a rocky point a good mile away.

"Whatta we do now?" Dinky wailed, as the tail end of the rowboat went out of sight.

"Wait'll I get my hands on that Harmon," Freddy muttered, shaking his pudgy fist in the direction of the shoreline. "Just let me get my hands around his neck just once, and I'll sure make his ears pop!"

"Seems to me like you had plenty a chance just now," Dinky observed.

"Yeah? Well, I just wasn't ready," Freddy grunted, as he took a sidewise swipe at a small rock and kicked it thirty feet into the water. "Oh boy!" he chortled, "When I get through with him, even Daphne won't recognize him."

Daphne is Harmon Muldoon's sister, and she's pretty sleek. She's even prettier than Stony Martin's girl-friend, Melissa Plunkett. And her teeth don't stick out in front, like Melissa's do.

"Oh boy! Oh boy!" Freddy muttered again through tightly pressed lips, as he ran up the narrow beach and took another vicious swipe at a larger rock. The rock didn't move, and Freddy hopped around in the sand holding his right foot in one hand and bellowing like a mad bull.

"Let's knock off the comedy and figure out what we're gonna do," Dinky said impatiently, as he plunked himself down in the sand and adopted the pose of *The Thinker*. "We're marooned, and nobody knows where we are," he added dramatically.

Both Freddy and Dinky can swim, but not very far; and the closest point of the shoreline was more than a half-mile away. Of course, Freddy can float forever, but he doesn't make much progress unless somebody pushes him.

"Maybe we could build a raft," Dinky mused.

"With what?" Freddy sneered. "We ain't even got an axe, and no nails or nothin'."

"We could build one if we had enough ingenuity," said Dinky.

"Injun what?"

"In-gen-oo-it-tee, stupid!"

"I never heard a that stuff. Will it float real good?"

"You fat dummy!" Dinky snorted, as he threw a handful of sand at Freddy's head. Freddy threw a handful right back and caught Dinky with his mouth open.

"Well, you're always such a big Injun expert, I thought maybe you had something real good in your noodle—like a birch bark canoe, or somethin'."

"How we gonna make a canoe, when we can't even make a raft?" Dinky sputtered, as he tried to get the sand out of his teeth. "Sometimes you make me sick."

"Well, we can't stay here forever," said Freddy. "Pretty soon it'll be lunch time, and I gotta eat."

"Whew!" said Dinky. "Is that all you ever think about? I can see you risin' up in your coffin and askin' for a sandwich before they bury you."

"At least I ain't skinny as you!" Freddy replied.

"C'mon. Let's take a walk around the island," said Dinky.

"Maybe we can find an old log that'll float, and we can drag it out into the water."

Half an hour later they flopped down on the sand again on the same stretch of beach where the rowboat had left them. There just wasn't anything loose on that island that would float. Freddy took his shoes off and worked his bare toes into the sand.

"Boy, that feels good. Hey! Why don't we build a fire and send up smoke signals? Somebody'll see 'em and come out and rescue us."

"Nuts!" said Dinky.

"Why not? I've seen you start a fire with nothin' at all. And you know all them Injun smoke signals, too."

"Nobody'll pay any attention to any smoke signals," said Dinky. "People are building campfires on these islands all the time, for picnics. We'd have to set the whole island on fire before it would attract attention."

"Maybe somebody would notice it if we built a big fire at night."

"I don't figure on spending the night here," said Dinky, as he jumped to his feet. "I just had an idea!"

From his pocket Dinky pulled a scuffed-up leather marble pouch, pulled the thong loose, and spilled the contents on the ground. Three beautiful agates, two steelys, and a small red-eye rolled into a crevice in the sand. A little shaking brought out two fish hooks, a ball of line, a GI can opener, and a bright metal object with a hole in it that looked like it might be some kind of whistle.

"What's that?" asked Freddy.

"That's a dog whistle."

"Whatta ya gonna do with it?"

"I'm gonna blow on it," said Dinky. And he did.

Freddy Muldoon squinted his eyes up into narrow slits. "I don't hear nothin'. Nothin' at all."

"You're not supposed to," said Dinky. "But a dog can hear it. Dogs have real good ears."

"Oh, you're real smart," said Freddy, "but there's just one thing wrong. I don't see no dogs around here."

"Wait and see!" said Dinky. And he kept blowing on the whistle until Freddy thought he had gone daft.

Back at Zeke Boniface's junkyard on the edge of town, there was the usual assortment of Saturday morning lookers and scavengers trying to find whatever it was they were looking for. Zeke was lying flat on his back in a hammock, under the shade of a corrugated tin roof, puffing on the stub of a cigar. His battered black bowler hat was tilted over his eyes just far enough so it would keep the glare out and still let him see Kaiser Bill, his German shepherd dog. Zeke didn't have to watch the customers. Kaiser Bill took care of that, and Zeke just watched Kaiser Bill.

Kaiser Bill was stretched out flat on his belly in the hot sun, with his jet black muzzle resting on his paws. The golden brown fur above his eyes was wrinkled into a soft frown, and his keen brown eyes shifted tirelessly back and forth, tracking the movements of every two-legged creature on the lot. Nobody ever left Zeke's junkyard without checking in at the hammock to haggle over the price of what he wanted to take with him, or at least to say 'goodbye'.

It was a normal Saturday morning. Or, so it seemed—until Zeke noticed a peculiar change in Kaiser Bill's behavior. The dog hadn't moved a muscle for fifteen minutes; but suddenly the coarse whiskers on his jowls fanned outward and stood erect, pointing slightly forward. Then the magnificent ears pricked up and rotated to the front. The wrinkles on his brow deepened into a frown of real concern, and he lifted his head from his paws and arched his neck. Then, like a shot, he was off across the junkyard; and with one great, scrambling leap he was over the seven-foot fence and off into the woods.

Zeke sat bolt upright and the hammock flipped violently, plopping him face-down into the dust. He picked himself up, beating the dust off his trousers with his black derby and spitting out the fragments of the cigar stub he had almost swallowed.

"What in tarnation got into him?" he sputtered, while a chorus of raucous laughter fell on his ears.

"Maybe he just remembered an important date!" one of the customers cried.

"Maybe he just heard Lassie was in town!"

"I'll bet he just wanted to get a manicure before the barbershop closed!" said another wiseacre.

Zeke got a lot of screamingly funny comments, but no offers of help to find out where Kaiser Bill went. He flopped his huge bulk into the hammock again, and lighted up a fresh cigar stub.

It was only fifteen minutes later that Dinky saw the dog plunge into the water from a point on the lake shore opposite the island. "C'mon, Kaiser! C'mon!" he shouted, clapping his hands as loudly as he could.

"Hey! That looks like Kaiser Bill!" said Freddy, jumping up and down.

"As usual, you take the cake," said Dinky. "What did you think I was blowing that whistle for?"

Soon Kaiser Bill galloped ashore on the tiny beach, spread his four feet far apart, and shook a spray of water twenty feet in both directions. Then he bounded toward Dinky, rose up on his rear legs and thumped his forepaws on Dinky's chest. Dinky ruffled his ears and kissed him on his black snout.

"Boy, am I glad to see you!" he said.

Kaiser Bill spun around twice, then flopped on his belly in the sand and lay there panting heavily, with his tongue hanging out of the left side of his mouth.

"I gotta admit you pulled a good one with that whistle," said Freddy, "but what do we do now? Now we got three of us marooned on this island."

"I didn't call him out here just for nothin'," said Dinky.

"Well, whatta we gonna do? Get on his back and ride him to shore?"

"Nope! He's gonna carry a message for us."

"Good idea! I suppose you got a pencil and a piece of paper?"

Dinky looked flustered for a moment. "No, I don't have a pencil," he admitted. "But, if you'll lend me your knife I can carve out a message on a piece of bark."

"You flunked out again," said Freddy. "I don't have a knife."

"You mean you came all the way out here without your knife?"

"I didn't know I was coming!" Freddy retorted. "Besides, where is *your* knife?"

"None of your business!" said Dinky. And he kicked a few stones into the water.

Freddy perched himself on a flat rock in the shade of a young maple and pulled a baloney sandwich out of his shirt. He was just unwrapping the wax paper from it when Dinky spun around at the sound and pointed a finger right at him.

"That's just what we need!" he cried.

"Whadda ya mean? This here hunk of paper?"

"No! I mean the whole sandwich. Paper and all."

"Nothin' doin'. If you want some lunch, you gotta bring your own."

"I don't want any lunch," said Dinky, "but we can use that sandwich to send a message."

"You must be nuts!"

"Listen! We could send that sandwich with Kaiser Bill, and Zeke would know it was one of your sandwiches and come looking for us."

"Now I know you're nuts!" said Freddy, biting a corner off the sandwich. "That big ball of fur would swallow it in one gulp before he got across the lake."

"He can't eat it if we tie it around his neck," Dinky reasoned.

"Too risky," said Freddy, taking another bite. "Besides, I need my lunch."

"You and your lunch!" Dinky fumed. "What would you rather be, a dead fat boy, or a live skinny one?"

"I'll have to think that over," Freddy answered, licking the mustard off his lips.

"Gimme that sandwich!" Dinky shouted, and he lunged straight at Freddy with all the fury his seventy-five pounds could muster. Freddy met him with a stiff arm right in the chest and he bounced back ten feet, sprawling full length in the sand. But he was up in a flash and threw a handful of sand right in Freddy's face. Freddy grabbed a handful of the stuff, himself, and poised to throw it—but it never left his hand. A deep-throated snarl stopped his hand in midair, and he found himself looking into the menacing eyes of Kaiser Bill.

Freddy retreated a step, holding the half-eaten sandwich high above his head. Kaiser Bill moved forward an equal distance, with the hair on his black saddle standing erect.

"Get outta here!" Freddy blustered, but his voice quavered and Kaiser Bill moved a step closer with his lips curled in another snarl.

"Call him off! Call him off!" Freddy pleaded.

"Give me the sandwich, first!"

"Okay! Okay! Come and get it. Quick!"

Dinky stepped between the two and took the remains of the sandwich from Freddy's hand. Kaiser Bill relaxed and trotted after Dinky, wagging his tail, as Dinky ran to retrieve the wax paper Freddy had tossed into the water.

"Now, let me have your shoelaces," Dinky said, as he started unlacing his own.

"What for?" Freddy wailed.

"So I can tie this sandwich around Kaiser's neck."

"What about that fishline you got in your pocket. Use that!"

"We might need that to catch fish with," Dinky said. "Now, give me your shoelaces."

"Go fish for 'em!" Freddy taunted.

Dinky snapped his fingers twice and Kaiser Bill

trotted over to stand spraddle-legged in front of Freddy.

"Okay! Okay!" Freddy grunted. "Call off your man-eater." And he started unlacing his shoes.

Dinky wrapped the remains of the baloney sandwich carefully, threaded the laces twice through the wax paper, and tied it securely around Kaiser Bill's neck.

"Go home, boy! Go!" Dinky commanded, with a firm pat on the dog's saddle. Kaiser Bill took a step toward the water, then looked back with a questioning frown. "Go boy! Go!" Dinky shouted, with a clap of his hands. "Go home!" Kaiser Bill bolted for the water and plunged into it, cutting a wake that pointed straight for the mainland shore. Nothing was visible from the island but a black snout, two ears folded to the rear, and a baloney sandwich. "Go, boy, go!" Dinky shouted, clapping his hands again.

"Yeah! Go, boy, go!" shouted Freddy, as he threw a stick that plopped into the water about ten feet from shore. Then he pulled another baloney sandwich from his shirt and sat down to eat it.

Back at the clubhouse in Jeff Crocker's barn, the rest of us were gathered around the big map of the county that hangs on one wall. Jeff and Henry were trying to lay out a search pattern for us that would cover the most likely places that Harmon's gang might be holding Freddy and Dinky. We had already been through a lot of arguments about how to proceed with the search; and Mortimer Dalrymple's suggestion that we simply make a frontal assault on Harmon's clubhouse in Egan's Alley had been voted down by a count of three to two. I was in favor of Mortimer's proposal; but Homer Snodgrass had sided with Jeff and Henry, who figured the clubhouse was too obvious a hiding place. Mortimer is always in favor of action, and Homer is always in favor of thinking things over a little longer.

"Maybe one of them has a transceiver with him," I suggested. "We ought to be monitoring the radio."

Jeff shook his head. "I'm sure Harmon would be smart enough to take it away from them," he observed.

Just then the buzzer on our intercom sounded. It was Zeke Boniface calling. "Let me talk to Freddy," he asked, when Henry answered the box.

"Freddy isn't here and we don't know where he is," Henry explained. "Have you seen him?"

"Nope! But I think Kaiser Bill has."

"What do you mean?"

"Well, this big baboon took off cross-country about an hour ago, and I couldn't stop him. He just came back, soaking wet, and he's got a baloney sandwich tied around his neck. I figured it might belong to Freddy. You know how he likes baloney."

"What kind of bread is it?"

"It's rye bread, with a lotta them black seeds in it."

"That's Freddy's alright! Boy, Zeke, you might have saved the day. We'll be down there in ten minutes."

"Okay! But is something wrong with Freddy?"

Henry ignored the question. "Hey, Zeke! You say this was tied around Kaiser Bill's neck?"

"Yeah!"

"What was it tied with?"

"Some old shoelaces, looks like."

"Hold onto them! We'll be at your place as quick as we can get there."

Ten minutes later we were all at Zeke's junkyard, where everything looked like "business as usual," except for Kaiser Bill. Instead of lying quietly in the sun, he was pacing restlessly up and down, now and then nuzzling the seat of Zeke's pants as he passed him. We looked at the baloney sandwich, and it was Freddy's, alright.

"Let me see the shoelaces," said Henry. Zeke pulled them out of his pocket, and Henry examined them carefully.

"Looks like you were right," said Jeff Crocker, looking over Henry's shoulder. "They sent us a message."

Sure enough, the shoelaces had been tied together in a series of knots, some double knots and some single. Henry stretched the string of knots out on the ground while he and Jeff decoded the message, scratching the letters out in the dirt.

"This is Morse code," Henry explained to Zeke. "The double knots are dashes and the single ones are dots."

Jeff had scratched the letters I-S-L in the dirt. "You sure that's Freddy's handwriting?" quipped Mortimer. "No! It looks more like Dinky's," Jeff shot right back. "Freddy makes fatter knots." After Henry had called out the last letter the word I-S-L-A-N-D appeared on the ground.

"They must be on an island somewhere," said Homer.

"Great deduction, Snodgrass! Great deduction!" said Mortimer, caustically.

"The only question is *where*," Jeff observed. "*What*

island are they on?"

"Probably Strawberry Lake," I ventured.

"But there's plenty of islands in the river, too. How we gonna search them all?" said Homer.

"We don't have to search them all," said Henry, in his usual matter-of-fact manner. "We have the answer right here."

"Oh, oh!" said Mortimer. "The great Mulligan has the magic answer, as usual."

"There's no magic to it at all," said Henry, pointing at Kaiser Bill. "Kaiser knows which island they're on. All we have to do is follow him."

And follow him we did. Zeke waved the baloney sandwich in front of Kaiser's nose and said, "Go, boy, go!," and off he went. Jeff and I had the job of following him cross-country, because we're both pretty good runners, and the rest of them piled into Zeke's old junk truck, Richard The Deep Breather. My job was to run like blazes and keep Kaiser Bill in sight so he wouldn't outdistance us. Jeff is bigger than I am, and can't run quite as fast; so it was up to him to keep up as best he could, and act as a radio relay to the truck so Henry could know where we were heading. Our two-way radios are pretty good; but you never can tell when a hill, or some dense woods, or a freak atmospheric disturbance is going to mask your transmission. So it's best to use a relay whenever you can to make sure your messages get through.

We needed it alright, because Kaiser Bill led me through everything you can imagine as he raced through swamps, woods, gullies, and over the crests of hills on a beeline toward the point on the lakeshore opposite the island where he had left Freddy and Dinky. Every time we'd pass some prominent landmark like a hill, or a big tree, or a rock pile, or an old tumble-down sheep shelter, I'd stop for a few seconds and pant out directions to Jeff on the radio. Sometimes he'd make me repeat them three or four times because I was so out of breath he couldn't understand me, and I'd get mad and shout things I shouldn't say on the air. But, somehow we managed to keep in communication, and Jeff scrambled on after me, and Zeke kept maneuvering Richard The Deep Breather through a network of back roads and old logging trails, trying to keep close to us.

At the lakeshore, Kaiser Bill scampered over pile after pile of huge boulders and fallen tree trunks lining the water's edge, and came to a stop in the middle of a small stretch of sandy beach. He stood poised like a pointer for a moment, with one foreleg crooked under his chest, and the black button of his nose sniffing the air in the direction of a rocky island. Then he pranced up the beach and back again, in a sort of stiff-legged canter, looking out toward the island, and then back at me. Then he planted both forepaws in the water and started lapping up huge gulps of the stuff. Then he went through the prancing act again.

I got the message, alright. He wanted me to swim out to the island with him, but I was too out of breath to move another inch. I slapped my thigh and called him over to me, and I petted him and ruffled the scruff of his neck. Then I flopped down in the sand and called Jeff on the radio.

"Hey, Jeff, I think we found the island," I gasped, without bothering about all that corny radio procedure you're supposed to use. "Roger! I read you. Stand by, Green One," Jeff answered. He can be so formal sometimes, it makes you sick.

In a few minutes Jeff was back on the air again, after checking with Henry. "Red One says to pull back off that beach and keep out of sight!" he told me.

"Keep out of sight? What's going on? Aren't we going to rescue Dinky and Freddy?"

"This is Red One. You have your orders, Green One! Do as you're told, and keep the messenger with you. And you better brush up on your radio procedure, too! You're giving away vital information. This is not a secure net. Over and out."

After all the running I had done, this hit me in the face like a wet towel. I pressed the "talk" button on my handset and cut loose with a big fat raspberry: "Pfffffrrrrrttttt! How do you like that information, oh Big Red Raspberry!" I shouted. "This is Green Apples signing off!" And I shut my radio off.

But I knew better than to disregard Henry's instructions. Henry sometimes moves in mysterious ways, but he almost always knows what he's doing. So I called Kaiser Bill back from the water's edge, and the two of us climbed a little way up the steep slope of the hill behind the beach and hid among the trees. It seemed like an hour, but it was probably only about fifteen minutes before I heard a rock crash through the trees and plop into the water about a hundred feet to our left. Kaiser Bill sprang to his feet and an explosive growl burst from his throat. I threw my arms around his neck and held him, and whispered in his ear to calm him down. Every muscle in his body was tensed, and I could feel him trembling under my grip. Suddenly he relaxed and I saw the figures of Henry and Jeff scrambling over the pile of boulders at one end of the little beach. They kept close to the tree line, and once they had gotten past the barrier of the rocks they darted into the cover of overhanging branches and ran toward Kaiser and me in a crouch, as though somebody was looking down the backs of their necks.

"Have you guys gone nuts?" I asked. "What's with all the commando stuff?"

"Henry figures if Freddy and Dinky are on that island, Harmon's gang must have it under surveillance," Jeff explained. "We don't want them to know that we've found out where they are."

"Why not? Is this a war, or somethin'?"

"You might call it that," said Henry, when he had caught his breath, "and we've got to teach Harmon and his gang a lesson."

I just sat there and watched as Henry and Jeff tied a plastic bag around Kaiser Bill's neck. It contained one of our two-way radios, a tiny signal transmitter like the ones used to track birds and small animals, a roll of tape, a knife, matches, and a note. The note told Dinky to tape the little transmitter somewhere in his huge mop of hair, so we would always know where they were if Harmon's gang took them off the island. If Harmon's gang did come back, they were to hide the radio somewhere on the island. Meanwhile, they were to stay where they were, and if they had to stay on the island all night we would send food and blankets to them after it got dark.

"I betcha Freddy will swim to shore before he waits that long for something to eat," I said.

"You might be right," Henry answered, "but it ought to be interesting to find out how much the love of food dominates his psychology." Henry is always the complete scientist. He looks at everything in life as just another experiment.

When the bag had been tied securely, I pointed to the island and said, "Go!" to Kaiser Bill. That was all he needed. He shot down the slope of the hill and plunged into the water. All you could see of him was the smooth, brown part of his head between his folded ears, and his black snout sticking out of the water as he paddled toward the island.

But Henry had been right. Kaiser Bill was no more than halfway to the island when we saw two figures in a small rowboat putting out from a small cove some distance to the south of us. Jeff trained his binoculars on the boat.

"That's Buzzy McCauliffe and Joe Turner," he said. "I guess they're going out to investigate."

They were heading for the island, alright, but Kaiser Bill was there far ahead of them. We decided to wait where we were and see what happened; but we couldn't see too much, because the boat went around to the far side of the island, where Kaiser Bill had gone. In a few minutes we saw it come back into view, however, and Jeff trained the glasses on it again.

"Well, I wonder what all that was about?" he mused. "There's still two guys in the boat, but Kaiser Bill is sitting up in the bow! Hey!—It's Freddy and Dinky! What gives?"

We found out in a few minutes. Freddy and Dinky pulled the boat in among the rocks below us, laughing their heads off. When Buzzy and Joe Turner had nosed up to the beach where Freddy and Dinky were sitting in the shade of a tree reading Henry's note, Kaiser Bill had dashed to the water's edge with his hair standing on end and bared his teeth.

"What's that dog doing here?" Buzzy shouted.

"He lives here!" Dinky shouted back.

"Will he bite?"

"Why don't you come on in and find out."

Joe Turner pulled the boat a little closer in, and Buzzy stood up in the bow as if to jump onto the beach. Fortunately he only pretended to, because Kaiser Bill let the boat get within about ten feet of shore, then lunged through the air straight at Buzzy. Buzzy toppled over backwards and splashed into the water with his arms flailing. Kaiser Bill's momentum carried him right into the boat, where he ended up with his wet nose sliding right up the back of Joe Turner's neck. Joe didn't even turn around to find out what had happened. He just dove over the stern of the boat and swam for dear life. His dive propelled the boat into shore with Kaiser Bill in complete command, a piece of Joe's shirt dangling from his jaws.

Dinky grabbed Kaiser Bill by the collar and held the boat. He and Freddy clambered into it, with Freddy at the oars and Dinky standing up in the prow with a growling Kaiser Bill under a firm grip.

"We just wanted to take you back to shore," Buzzy sputtered, standing waist-deep in the water.

"Tell it to the Marines!" Freddy taunted.

"Thanks, but we can make it okay," Dinky added. They were still shouting wisecracks and laughing as Freddy pulled out of sight around the end of the island.

When Dinky had finished describing what had happened, we pulled the rowboat back in among the trees, slipped it in between two huge boulders, and covered it with brush. Then we took off to where Zeke was waiting with the truck.

We all went back to the clubhouse, where Henry spent fifteen minutes leaning back against the wall on his piano stool, gazing up into the roof rafters, while the rest of us played mumblety-peg on the barn floor. Kaiser Bill was stretched out on his stomach right in front of the door, gnawing on a huge bone from Mrs. Crocker's kitchen. Mortimer is usually the champ at mumblety-peg, but this time I won three games from him before the front legs of Henry's stool hit the floor and we all turned to find out what brilliant idea the great mind had come up with this time. But Henry didn't say anything for a while. He just sat there wiping the lenses of his horn-rimmed glasses clean. Finally he put them back on his nose and looked at all of us as though he hadn't realized we were there.

"What do we do now, oh High Mogul?" I asked him.

"We've got to get a message to Harmon," he answered, "and you're going to take it, Charlie."

"What are we gonna tell them?"

"We're gonna scare the pants off them," said Henry. "At last, I have Harmon right where I want him. He fell into this beautifully."

"Fell into what?" I asked.

"Never mind," said Henry, "but it wasn't any accident that Freddy and Dinky were here in the clubhouse this morning with the door unlocked."

Henry wrote out a note for me to take up to Memorial Point. It said

> IF FREDDY AND DINKY AREN'T BACK AT OUR CLUBHOUSE BY FOUR O'CLOCK THIS AFTERNOON, WE'LL REPORT THEIR DISAPPEARANCE TO THE POLICE. THANKS FOR LEAVING THE TAPE WITH YOUR VOICE ON IT.
>
> MULLIGAN

"Why didn't we tell the police in the first place?" Homer asked.

"You know I wouldn't do a thing like that," Henry replied. "It would spoil all the fun. But Harmon doesn't know that."

Then Henry pulled Dinky and Freddy aside and gave them some secret instructions, and sent them packing with Kaiser Bill trotting alongside. Homer and I got on our bicycles and pedaled out to Memorial Point, where we put Henry's note under a rock behind the old Civil War cannon. We rode back down the trail a bit, then hid our bicycles and circled back through the brush to hide in the bushes behind the clearing where the cannon and the statues stand. Pretty soon we saw Speedie Brown, one of the best tree climbers in Harmon's gang, come swinging down out of a big oak tree. He got the note from under the rock, read it, and stuffed it in his pocket. Then he pulled his bicycle out of the bushes and took off down the road.

"I'm sure he's heading for Harmon's clubhouse," Henry said, when we reported in on the radio. "We've got that covered. You go out to the lake and see if he shows up there, where Buzzy and Joe Turner were supposed to be watching the island."

Harmon was in for a hectic afternoon. Henry's note must have scared him, because he and Stony Martin did show up at the cove on the lakeshore about thirty minutes later. Harmon looked worried. He kept looking at his watch while he stumbled around through the trees and bushes hollering for Buzzy and Joe.

"Hey! Here's their radio and their lunches!" Stony cried. "They must be around here somewhere."

"I told those fatheads to keep that radio with them at all times," Harmon blustered. "No wonder we couldn't get any answer from them."

"You know what?" said Stony.

"What?" said Harmon.

"I don't see no boat!"

"Yeah! You know what?"

"What?"

"I don't see one neither!" said Harmon.

They both walked down to the water's edge with their hands on their hips and rubber-necked around the shoreline.

"I bet those lunkheads are out there on that island fat-cattin' with them other kids," said Harmon.

"If they are, we oughtta cut their hair off!" said Stony.

Harmon cupped his hands around his mouth and shouted as loud as he could. The echo came back across the lake, but nothing else. Then Stony tried it. It was easy to see Harmon was getting madder and madder, and soon they were both hollering at the top of their lungs.

Finally, two figures appeared on the near side of the island, waving their arms. Harmon swung his arm in a wide arc toward the lakeshore, and pumped his right arm up and down. But the two figures on the island just shook their heads and waved back.

"What are those ninnies doing, waving their arms like that?"

"I think they're trying to tell you something," said Stony.

"Brilliant, Martin, brilliant!" said Harmon. "Now, hand me your shirt."

Harmon took off his own shirt too, and with the one Stony handed him he started making wig-wag signals toward the island. Soon the shirts of Buzzy McCauliffe and Joe Turner were sending signals in reply.

"They say they don't have a boat, and they want us to come get them," Harmon snorted.

"What happened to the boat?" Stony asked.

"I don't know, knucklehead. When we get 'em in here we'll find out."

"Great!" said Stony. "I'll just take my shoes off, so they don't get wet, and walk over there."

"Look! We gotta find out what's going on," said Harmon, "and we gotta get those guys off that island. Now use your noodle!"

"What about that old tree trunk over there? We could push that into the water and paddle out to the island with it."

"Good idea!" said Harmon. "I'll help you push it in."

"Thanks a whole bunch!" said Stony.

The two of them grunted and struggled with the tree trunk while Homer and I sat in our hiding place in the bushes and tried to keep from laughing out loud. When they finally had it in the water, Stony stripped down to his shorts and waded out to the log.

"Come on! Get your duds off," he said. "You're the one that's in a hurry!"

"Look, lunkhead, somebody's got to stay here and guard your clothes. Now, get going! We don't have much time."

Stony splashed into the water, grabbed one end of the log and started kicking furiously. The huge log inched forward slowly, and Stony steered it toward the island. It took him better than fifteen minutes to reach the island, and about the same time to get back with Buzzy and Joe kicking along with him, their clothes and shoes piled on top of the log. Harmon had been stomping up and down the shore, gnawing his knuckles and looking at his watch every two minutes.

"Okay! What have you meatheads been up to?" he demanded, before they were even out of the water.

Buzzy tried to explain how Freddy and Dinky had commandeered their boat and made off with it. He and Joe were jumping up and down, trying to dry off enough to get back into their clothes.

"This is a fine mess you've gotten us into!" Harmon moaned. "I shoulda known better than to let two pumpkinheads like you handle it. Imagine letting two punk kids like that take your boat away from you."

"It wasn't them two kids, it was that big dog," Joe Turner argued. "He's a real monster. Look! He took half my shirt off!"

"Ouch!" cried Buzzy McCauliffe, jumping three feet in the air and clapping one hand to the seat of his pants. "Something bit me!"

"Sure it did!" said Harmon, backing away from him. "Your pants are swarmin' with big red ants. That log you put 'em on is lousy with 'em."

"Them's fire ants!" said Joe Turner. "Ouch! I got 'em too!"

"So that's it!" cried Stony Martin. "The water brought them swarmin' outa that log, and you saw 'em. That's why you didn't want to help me push that log out to the island."

"Shut up!" said Harmon. "Somebody's gotta use his brains around here. Now, let's get back to the clubhouse. We gotta find out what happened to those two kids."

I reported in to Henry on the radio while Harmon and his gang scrambled up the hill to the place where they had left their bicycles. Buzzy McCauliffe and Joe Turner, well in the lead, looked like two whirling dervishes on hot coals.

"Okay!" said Henry. "Freddy and Dinky are watching their clubhouse from Blaisdell's barn. Follow after Harmon until you're sure that's where they're going, and let me know. After that you can get down to the freight yards. We may need your help. But stay out of sight, unless I call you."

"Wilco! This is Rodger the Lodger signing off!" I said, and Homer and I took off up the hill to follow Harmon.

When Harmon and his entourage pedaled up Egan's Alley a little later, Freddy and Dinky were peeking out through the dust-covered windows of Blaisdell's barn, a little way down the alley from Stony Martin's garage where they have their clubhouse. Harmon was just getting off his bicycle when Dinky quietly opened the door of the barn about a foot, and whispered in Kaiser Bill's ear.

"Go get your bone, Kaiser! Get your bone!" and he slapped him smartly on the hindquarters.

Kaiser Bill shot through the door and darted up the alley so fast that Joe Turner had to turn the handlebars of his bicycle hard-over to get out of his way, and he ended up sprawled in the dust of the alley.

"That's him! That's him!" he shouted as he went down.

"Yeah!" cried Buzzy McCauliffe, pointing at the cloud of dust just rounding the corner. "That's the dog that was on the island. Follow him! Follow him! I betcha he knows where Fat Freddy and his friend are."

"Where'd he come from?"

"I dunno. He just came runnin' up the alley," Joe sputtered. "But he was with Fatty and Skinny on that island, and I bet he's chasin' after them right now. Go get him!"

"Okay! Okay!" Harmon blurted. "You two mutton-heads stay here with Speedie. Stony and I'll take care of this." And Harmon was back on his bicycle and chewing gravel in no time, with Stony pedaling after him.

They didn't know where they were going, but Kaiser Bill did. When they caught sight of him after they had turned the corner, he was heading straight down Railroad Avenue toward the freight yards. It was down-hill all the way, and they managed to gain on him some, until they got to the freight yards, where Railroad Avenue comes to a dead end. Kaiser Bill took the fence in one bound without breaking stride, and Harmon and Stony dumped their bicycles there and clambered over the fence after him. They had quite a job keeping him in sight, because Kaiser Bill didn't bother running around the ends of the strings of freight cars that were parked in the yards. He knew where his soup bone was hidden and he meant to get it. He darted under car after car, picking his way through the maze of sidings with his nose. Harmon and Stony scrambled after him, knocking their heads on tie rods and barking their shins on the steel rails.

Finally Kaiser Bill dashed across an open stretch between tracks and leaped through the open door of an empty red boxcar. Harmon and Stony came puffing along about twenty seconds later and climbed in after him. They were no sooner inside than Jeff Crocker and Mortimer Dalrymple popped out from behind the door of the next boxcar. Jeff put his fingers to his lips and cut loose with a sharp, piercing whistle. Kaiser Bill appeared at the door of the red boxcar with Mrs. Crocker's soup bone held firmly in his jaws. Jeff clapped his hands and Kaiser Bill jumped to the ground. Jeff slammed the door of the boxcar shut, and Mortimer jumped up and shot the locking pin home. Then they cleared out of there, with Kaiser Bill trotting along behind them, drooling all over the soup bone.

I felt a little sorry for Harmon and Stony, trapped in that boxcar. But I guess they got no more than they deserved. And they weren't quite alone. When they felt the first grinding jerk of the boxcar, as the freight train pulled out of the yards about half an hour later, they heard the voice of Henry Mulligan brought to them through the courtesy of Jeff and Mortimer, who had taped a handset to the roof of the car.

"This is Captain Mulligan," said Henry, as the rest of us rolled on the floor of Jeff's barn with our stomach muscles aching from laughter. "We welcome you aboard, and hope that your trip will be comfortable. We will be flying at an altitude of approximately five hundred and forty feet above sea level, and at a speed of about 18 knots. We have a tail wind of about three knots, but we don't expect that will help much. Our next stop will be Cobb's Junction, and we expect to let down there in about three hours. Have a pleasant trip. Thank you."

I could just see Harmon and Stony kicking the sides

of the boxcar and shaking their fists at the handset taped to the roof. I imagine one of them probably jumped and grabbed it, and smashed it against the wall before Henry even got finished. But we didn't care. Dinky was lying on the clubhouse floor with his head propped up on Kaiser Bill's broad back, with a contented smile on his face. Kaiser Bill was gnawing on his soup bone, and every time Freddy cast an envious glance toward it, Kaiser Bill would growl at him.

Harmon and Stony had to call their folks from Cobb's Junction, and they didn't get home until midnight. But they didn't dare tell anyone the true story of how they happened to get there.

Anyway, nobody ever tried to kidnap a member of The Mad Scientists' Club again.

The Mad Scientists' Club by Bertrand Brinley
A strange sea monster appears on the lake… a fortune is unearthed from an old cannon… a valuable dinosaur egg is stolen. Watch out as the seven Mad Scientists of Mammoth Falls turn their town upside down! Ages 8-12.

David and the Phoenix by Edward Ormondroyd
David and his new friend, the Phoenix, fly to various adventures and misadventures with mythical beings and an ill-intentioned scientist, until the Phoenix realizes that destiny calls. Ages 8-12.

Time at the Top by Edward Ormondroyd
After returning home from school, Susan Shaw takes her usual ride up the elevator and unusual things begin to happen. She finds herself in a strange time and place where she meets two new friends. Ages 8-12. Coming in 2003.

The Shy Stegosaurus of Cricket Creek by Evelyn Sibley Lampman
Joan and Joey Brown went hunting for dinosaur fossils and instead found a real dinosaur, genus stegosaurus! George (as they called him) was a loyal friend, helping the twins raise money for their mother's ranch. Ages 8-12.

TAL, His Marvelous Adventures with Noom-Zor-Noom
by Paul Fenimore Cooper
The story of a little orphan boy, Tal, and the adventures that befell him on the amazing journey to the land of Troom, accompanied by the wise old man, Noom-Zor-Noom, and his talking donkey Millitinkle. Written by the great-grandson of James Fenimore Cooper. Ages 8-12.

TWIG story and pictures by Elizabeth Orton Jones
Twig was an ordinary little girl who found an empty tomato can with pictures of bright red tomatoes round it. When it was upside down, it looked like a house just the right size for a fairy! This is the story of what happened in and around that house one magical Saturday afternoon. Ages 6-10.

Big Susan story and pictures by Elizabeth Orton Jones
The Doll family awaits the Wonderful Night when all dolls come alive at Christmas, when they can move and speak without help from Susan. A different sort of Christmas story to be enjoyed at any time of the year. Ages 6-10.

MORE

PURPLE HOUSE PRESS

CLASSICS

The Space Child's Mother Goose by Frederick Winsor
Only a few years ago we walked on solid earth. Today (1950s) we whirl through space. Space is big, it is not cozy. But with these verses, cheerfulness breaks in. Suddenly, science seems more merry and space seems to feel a little more like home. All ages.

For Younger Readers

Mr. Pine's Purple House story and pictures by Leonard Kessler
Learn how Mr. Pine cleverly solves the problem of living on a street with too many white houses, as he dares to be different! Ages 3-8.

Mr. Pine's Mixed-up Signs story and pictures by Leonard Kessler
Mr. Pine paints all new signs for Little Town, but loses his glasses. Pure chaos results after he puts the signs up anyway! How does Mr. Pine solve the problem of all those mixed-up signs? Ages 3-8.

Ann Likes Red by Dorothy Z. Seymour
Meet Ann, an independent little girl who knows what she likes. Red! Red! Red! Ages 3-6.

The Duchess Bakes A Cake by Virginia Kahl
A colorful tale of a Duchess, a Duke and their family of daughters. One day the Duchess decides to make *a lovely light luscious delectable cake*, and adds the yeast six times for good measure – Oh No! Ages 3-8.

Night of the Moonjellies by Mark Shasha
Young Mark spends a busy day helping out at his Gram's seaside hot dog stand and then sails off for a promised surprise to find a sea full of shimmering moonjellies. Ages 3-8.

Miss Twiggley's Tree by Dorothea Warren Fox
Funny Miss Twiggley lived in a tree, with a dog named Puss and a color tv. She did what she liked and she liked what she did. But when company came, Miss Twiggley hid! Ages 3-8. Coming fall 2002.